THE 1970s

Arguments

1990s

1980s

1970s

1960s

1950s

1940s

1930s

1920s

1910s

1900s

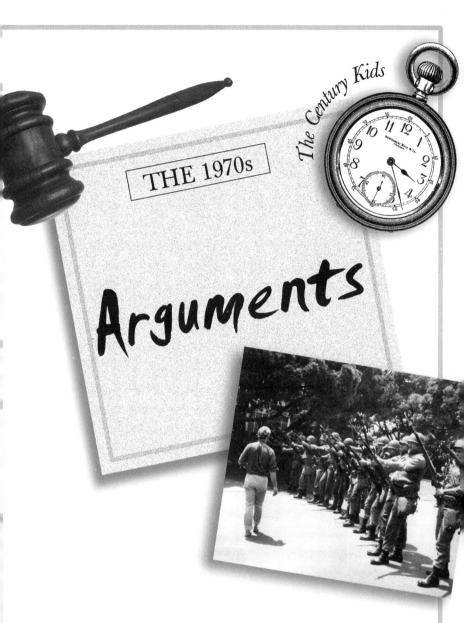

The Century Kids

THE 1970s

Arguments

by **Dorothy and Tom Hoobler**

The Millbrook Press • *Brookfield, Connecticut*

Photographs courtesy of Private collection: p. 7; Library of Congress:
p. 11 (#LC-USZ6 1232); H. Armstrong Roberts: pp. 12, 15, 30;
Underwood Photo Archives, S.F.: pp. 20, 26, 36, 62, 69, 99, 106, 116;
Bison Archives: p. 34; FPG International: pp. 37, 46; AP/Wide
World Photos: p. 38; Anne Canevari Green: p. 82; Corbis: pp. 111
(© Bettmann), 136 (© Wally McNamee); Woodfin Camp & Associates:
p. 114 (© George Hall); Marshall Field's: p. 138.

Primer, p. 25 by Lorraine Schneider. Courtesy of Elisa Kleven

To Jane Hoobler

Library of Congress Cataloging-in-Publication Data
Hoobler, Dorothy.
The 1970s : arguments / by Dorothy and Tom Hoobler.
p. cm.–(The century kids)
Summary: America's involvement in Vietnam adds to the
seemingly constant arguing in the Vivante family, whose
cousins are among a group of people who have dropped
out to live in a commune in Arizona.
ISBN 0-7613-1607-8 (lib. bdg.)
1. Vietnamese Conflict, 1961-1975–Juvenile fiction. [1. Vietnamese
Conflict, 1961-1975–Fiction. 2. Communal living–Fiction.
3. Family life–Fiction. 4. Cousins–Fiction. 5. Italian Americans–
Fiction.] I. Hoobler, Thomas. II. Title.
PZ7.H76227   Aaf 2002
[Fic]–dc21   2001030292

Published by The Millbrook Press, Inc.
2 Old New Milford Road
Brookfield, Connecticut 06804
www.millbrookpress.com

ONE

An Ending

FEBRUARY 27, 1970

IT WOULD BE NICE TO BE BURIED HERE, LUCY thought. At least as long as you were dead, and *had* to be buried. Lucy was eleven and hoped that wouldn't happen to her for a long time yet.

The grave she was looking at rested on the side of a hill overlooking a lake. Lake Chohobee was its name. And all around the grave stood evergreen trees that must look spectacular when they were covered with snow, in the winter. They must get a lot of snow here in Maine, Lucy thought.

She shivered. She'd made herself cold, just thinking about it. That was the sort of thing Lucy had learned not to tell other people. How she could imagine herself being somewhere else, so that for a moment she really felt as if she were there.

Mama knew she could do that. She was always warning Lucy: "Don't be so strange. You'll wind up alone and sitting by yourself." Mama had an aunt who wound up like that, and she was afraid Lucy had inherited the family trait.

Thinking about the grave, however, gave Lucy an idea for a poem. She got out her notebook. She was sitting in the back row of folding chairs that had been set up on the hill, so she was pretty sure nobody would see her. Everybody else was facing the grave, waiting for the service to begin.

She tried to think of the name of the person who was being buried, but she had forgotten. It was one of the Aldriches, she knew. A friend of her Grandpop Rocco's.

That was why Lucy and practically everybody else in the Vivanti family were here. Three days ago, they had been sitting down to dinner at the big table in Rocco's Famous, which was what everybody called their family's restaurant. An argument had broken out even before they finished with the antipasto. This time, it was between Lucy's father and his brother, Uncle Tony.

Uncle Tony had said something like, "This olive oil isn't as good as we were getting last year."

And Lucy's father got hot under the collar, because of course he was responsible for buying the olive oil. But instead of saying that the olive oil was the same as it ever was, he said, "At least we didn't have to throw half of it out—like we did with the fish."

As everybody at the table knew, Uncle Tony's job was buying fish for the restaurant.

That's how it began, but as Lucy's mother often said, "If it's not one thing, it's another." Lucy knew that both her father and Uncle Tony felt they should be

Lucy

the one running the restaurant. And to settle the dispute, Grandpop Rocco had put their sister, Aunt Gabriella, in charge.

Of course, nobody but Rocco was *really* in charge. Grandmama had more or less retired, and kept telling Rocco they should spend the winter in Florida. But Grandpop wouldn't let go. Aunt Gabriella ran the kitchen, but every night Rocco still held court in the dining room. He went from table to table, chatting with old friends and making sure that new customers got the best meal they ever had in their lives.

Of course, Dad and Uncle Tony weren't the only ones who argued. Mike and Art, Uncle Tony's sons, were always at each other's throats about the Vietnam War. Lucy's mom fought with

Aunt Irene. Rocco fought with just about anybody. Lucy was always surprised whenever she went to somebody else's house for dinner and there wasn't any yelling and shouting at the table.

Usually, the fights ended when Grandmama shouted for everybody to shut up. But that night, the phone rang and because of the argument, nobody heard it. So Gabriella had picked it up in the kitchen. When she came out to the dining room, everybody stopped talking. Gabriella had a look on her face that made Lucy think she better run down to church and light a candle.

"Pop," Gabriella said quietly. "That was Charley Norman."

Everybody looked blank, because they hadn't heard the phone. "Charley?" said Rocco. "He's in the kitchen?"

"No, on the *phone*," said Gabriella. "If you didn't all yell all the time, you would have heard it."

"I never yell," said Aunt Irene, and Lucy thought another fight was about to break out.

"Charley said his mother just died, Pop," said Lucy.

Peggy. That was her name. Lucy remembered now, as she sat in her chair trying to think of a poem. Not many words rhymed with Peggy. Leggy did, but that wouldn't fit into the kind of poem Lucy wanted to write.

Somebody turned on the microphone that had been set up next to the grave. It made a loud squeal and Lucy looked up. Grandpop Rocco stood there, looking at the microphone the way he did when he found a piece of cork floating in somebody's wineglass.

He turned the microphone off. "Can everybody hear me without this thing?" he said. Even though there were a lot of people—at least a hundred—everybody nodded. Grandpop's voice carried even to the last row, and Lucy waved so he'd know.

"I'm not such a great speaker," Grandpop said.

Lucy smiled as she went back to the poem. He always said that, because he still had a slight Italian accent. But she noticed that whenever Grandpop talked, everybody listened. Something about him made you think what he said was important. Or at least true. And you'd better pay attention.

"But I owe a lot to my friend Peggy Aldrich," Grandpop went on. "In fact, she saved my life."

Lucy sat up to hear better. See, right there, he'd said something that sounded important. This was a story she hadn't heard before. She knew about the stolen necklace that Lorraine—and Charley Norman—had found, because on a wall at the restaurant there was a yellowed newspaper clipping that told all about it. But saving Grandpop's life? How did that happen? Maybe on the boat when he came over from Italy. He never talked about that.

"I was running from the cops," Rocco said. Then he smiled, because everybody listening started to murmur in surprise. "Well," he added, "it was a strike in the textile mills and the cops were supposed to break it up."

Lucy was listening more carefully now. It was funny to think of Grandpop running from the cops. Policemen often came to eat at his restaurant. One of his best friends was Chicago's chief of police.

Rocco waved his hand. "Anyway," he said, "Peggy did a lot more than that. After saving my life, she took me home." He gestured to the big house at the top of the hill. Lucy hadn't known Grandpa lived here. Just imagine how cool that must have been.

"She even bought me a suit," said Grandpop. "And a pair of shoes. The first brand-new ones I ever had in my life."

Grandpop paused and took a step back from the microphone. He rubbed his left hand across his eyes. If Lucy didn't know better, she would almost have thought he was crying. But he would never cry, and certainly not about a pair of shoes.

"Maybe I ought to let somebody else talk now," Rocco muttered after stepping forward again.

"No, no," people called out. "Go on."

"Well, I just wanted to say, Peggy didn't do that because I was anything special." He looked around. "I'm glad none of you can see me the way I was then—a dirty little kid fresh off the boat."

Lucy smiled. Maybe that was the reason why Grandpop was always so neat and sharp, careful to have his tie knotted just right and his shoes shined every day.

"No," Grandpop said loudly, looking at somebody in the front row of seats. Lucy stood up to see, but she couldn't tell who it was.

Rocco as a boy

"No," he repeated. "Peggy was the kind of person who helped everyone. I'm not going to make a list here, because we'd be here all day if I did." He looked at the audience again. "Some of you here . . . she helped you, whenever she could."

He spread his hands. "I never thanked her for everything she did for me. You know how that is. We never say the things we ought to say the most. So here I am now to say them. Peggy, the world isn't as good a place without you."

As he turned away from the microphone, people clapped loudly. Finally somebody else stood up and came forward. Lucy recognized her. It was

Nell

Nell Aldrich, Peggy's sister. She used to be a movie star about a million years ago, and then had a TV program too. But Lucy had never seen it, because it had gone off the air.

Nell still looked pretty good, Lucy thought. You could tell she had been somebody important like a star by her clothes. She had on a black dress with lace trim. Other women were wearing dresses like it, but none of them fit just right, the way Nell's did. Lucy's mama had worked in a dress shop before she married Daddy, and she taught Lucy how to recognize good clothes.

"Thank you, Rocco," Nell said, smiling at him. "I know what you said is true, because I was there too, remember?" Her eyes twinkled as if she were teasing him.

"In fact, if I recall correctly," she went on, "I was the one who pushed Peggy into the path of the policeman who was chasing you." People laughed at that. Lucy could see why. The thought of this gentle old lady doing something like that seemed ridiculous.

Nell wagged her finger at him playfully. "And don't forget, Rocco, I wanted you to stay here, but you ran off to Chicago."

More laughter from the front rows. Lucy was puzzled. Why wouldn't Grandpop want to stay here? This place was like . . . a fairyland.

"But you're right about Peggy," Nell said. "She helped everybody. Most of all she helped me. She wrote some of my best movies. And you know, she could have had her own career as an actress. To tell you all the truth, she was better than I was."

Nell paused and looked around. "Why didn't she continue with her own acting career? I asked her that once, but she wouldn't tell me. I suspect it was because when you're onstage, or in front of a movie camera, you're doing what someone else has thought up for you, speaking someone else's words. The writer's words. And that's why Peggy turned to writing. She wanted to be in charge."

Lucy felt a little thrill. Being a writer was what *she* wanted to be. She wished now that she'd met Peggy. Nell went on speaking, but Lucy had some more ideas for her poem, and started to write.

She didn't look up again until she realized everybody else was standing. People were starting to sing. It wasn't a song Lucy recognized, so she just listened.

Then, still singing, people started to walk up to the grave. Lucy felt afraid, and she looked around for some way to get out of that. But her mother turned and beckoned for her to follow.

As she got closer, Lucy saw that people were dropping red roses on top of the coffin. A chubby man was handing them out. Lucy recognized him. He was Charley Norman, Peggy's son. He still came to Rocco's restaurant from time to time.

After they passed the grave, people stopped to shake Nell's hand and say a few words. Next to her stood a young man who looked just like Charley, only younger.

Lucy took one of the roses—and on an impulse, she tore from her notebook the page that held the poem. As she came to the grave, she folded it and let it drop with the rose. It fluttered down like a baby bird that couldn't quite fly yet.

Nobody noticed, she thought. Nell and the others were looking over Lucy's head at the next person in line. She turned out of curiosity, and saw a man on crutches who was only a little taller than Lucy herself.

Just as she turned, one of his crutches caught the edge of a rock in the grass. He stumbled forward, and Lucy put out her hand to steady him. He smiled and nodded his thanks.

"Hello, Dick," Nell said to the man. "It was good of you to come all the way from Los Angeles."

"Peggy made the trip when my father died last year," said Dick. "And besides . . . she did a lot for us after Father's stroke."

"I know she was happy to write another movie," Charley said. "And when she thought of a hero who was confined to a wheelchair, it seemed a natural for Harry. She was glad you and he agreed to do the film."

Lucy blurted out, "Was that *Man on Wheels*? I saw that. It was so sad, but it made you feel good anyway."

Dick

They all smiled at her. "My father would be glad to hear that," Dick said.

"Harry Aldrich was your father?" she asked. Then she realized it was a little rude to sound so surprised.

"Yes," he said with a smile to let her know she wasn't the first person to be surprised.

"And you must be one of Rocco's grandchildren," said Nell.

Lucy nodded. "I'm Lucy Vivanti," she said.

"You're one of Leo's girls."

"And a writer like Peggy," Dick added.

"Is that so?" asked Nell. "How do you know, Dick?"

Lucy gave him a look, hoping he wouldn't reveal what he had seen.

And he didn't. "She's carrying a notebook," he said. He gave Lucy a wink.

"We'll see you all up at the house later," said Nell.

Dick moved faster on his crutches than Lucy would have thought possible. She had to run every few steps to keep up with him. "Thanks for not telling them I put my poem on the coffin," she said.

"Nothing wrong with that," Dick replied. "I think Peggy would have liked it. Where did you meet her?"

Lucy was embarrassed. "I never did, really," she said. "I just listened to what people said about her, and it seemed like such a nice place to be buried, you know?" She stopped, thinking that he must find that a dumb thing to say.

"You know," Dick said, "that was exactly what I was thinking. I wondered if my father would rather have been buried here, instead of Los Angeles."

"From the movie he made," said Lucy, "I think Los Angeles would have been better."

"You do? Why?"

"Oh . . . in the movie it seemed like he had all this energy. Even though he was in a wheelchair, and was old, and all. Los Angeles is more his kind of place."

Dick nodded. "You know," he said, "I think you're right."

"Are you going to make another movie?" Lucy asked.

He nodded. "I wanted to make a real-life movie. Peggy and I talked about doing one before she died. The country has gone through so much turmoil in the past few years. Peggy and I thought somebody should take a close look at it. Maybe visit some families and see how it's affected them."

"When you say turmoil . . .", Lucy said, ". . . you mean like all the arguments over the Vietnam War?"

"That's one of the things, yes."

"Oh, let me tell you about my family."

Another Kind of Family

APRIL 6, 1970

AT THE TASK MEETING ON SUNDAY, SAM volunteered to hoe the field of pepper plants, a job he usually avoided. Agatha had nodded with approval, and penciled his name on the field list. Agatha said she thought Sam showed signs of what she called "a renewed dedication to the spirit of cooperation."

Sam's mother knew better. She had given Sam a wry smile across the council fire from her seat next to Agatha. It was hard to fool Mom, Sam thought. She understood that the pepper field was right next to the dirt road that led from the commune to town. The mailbox was up there, and this

Sam

was the week when the new issue of *Popular Electronics* usually arrived.

Sam's dad had subscribed to it, but he was gone now. If somebody else got to the mailbox first, they would probably take the magazine to Agatha. Then the communal council would discuss whether it was or wasn't a positive contribution to the commune's welfare.

Every time *Popular Electronics* arrived, it caused a heated discussion. There were some members of the commune who felt that they shouldn't even *have* electricity if the commune was going to be self-sufficient.

It had been Sam's dad who hooked them up to the electric lines in the first place. Sam remembered the night when Dad was trying to read a book by the light from beeswax candles. The members of the commune had made the candles, but something was wrong with the wax. The candles kept flickering and going out. Finally, Sam's dad had stood up, snapped the book shut, and said, "That's enough!"

Since he went right to bed after that, Sam figured he meant that was enough reading for tonight. But the next morning, Dad had walked the two miles to town and come back with some wire and other stuff from the hardware store.

"That's electrical equipment," Agatha said when she saw it.

"Right again," said Dad. He and Agatha often had what Mama called "discussions." Sam thought they were more like arguments, but nobody in the commune was supposed to argue so that couldn't be right.

"There is no electricity here at the commune," said Agatha. She meant that the council had decided not to allow any.

"Actually, there *is*," said Dad. He pointed to the power lines that were strung on poles from the state road. "This used to be a ranch, and they had plenty of electricity. All I have to do is connect it up again."

Agatha sniffed and went off. By the time she called the communal council together, Dad had finished the job. And what was the first thing he got running? Not the electric lights in their cabin, which was the whole reason he had decided to bring electricity to the commune.

No, he brought power to the electric pump at the old ranch house, which meant they could get water just by turning a faucet. Sam watched the faces of the council members as Dad showed it to them. All of them knew what hard work it was to pump water out of the ground by hand. It was fun, a little, if all you wanted was a cup of water to drink. But if you needed enough to take a bath in, or wash clothes, it wasn't fun at all.

Dad was smart. When he defended the electric project in front of the council, he said, "Electricity is just as natural as anything else we use—water from the stream, sunshine, beeswax, the food we grow." A majority of the council agreed and decided it was OK to have electricity.

Afterward, when he and Dad were alone, Sam said, "You should be elected head of the council instead of Agatha. You'd be lots better than her."

Dad got that funny smile on his face that meant he knew something Sam didn't. "That's true," he said, "But would it be better for *me* if I were the leader? Would it be better for Agatha if she weren't?"

When Dad asked questions like that, he never answered them. He just let Sam think about them. Sam finally decided the answer to both questions was supposed to be no, but he couldn't figure out why.

Fortunately, Dad gave better explanations when Sam asked about electricity. Sam learned how to make connections and where to turn the power off while you were working. The rest was pretty easy.

A couple of months later, the power company sent a truck out to the commune. A man in a uniform got out and started to inspect the power line. Sam's dad came over to greet him, and Sam tagged along.

"You're not supposed to hook up the power on your own," the man said. "It's too dangerous."

"We didn't see any need to bother you," said Sam's dad. "It was such a small job."

"Another thing," the man said, following the new lines that led to the cabins the commune members had built, "you've got to pay for the electricity. Didn't you get the bills we sent?"

"Well, we haven't got much money," Sam's dad said with a smile. "We really didn't think you'd miss the electricity. We don't use much."

The man gave him a funny look. "That's why we have meters," he said. They went inside one of the cabins and inspected the wall plug Sam's dad had installed. "Nice job," the man said, "You ever work as an electrician?"

"I took electrical engineering at Cal Berkeley," said Sam's dad.

"You did?" The man seemed surprised. "So what are you doing . . ." He looked around. ". . . out here with *these* people?"

"Looking for a better way," said Sam's dad.

In the end, Sam's dad gave the man some homemade raspberry preserves on a slice of freshly baked bread. The man agreed to take a couple of jars of the preserves. In return, he was going to fix up the meter so the commune wouldn't have to pay its back bill.

"Just this one time," the man said. "In the future, you'll have to pay."

"Sure," said Sam's dad.

"Your wife makes great preserves," the man added.

"Oh, I make the preserves myself," said Sam's dad. That brought another funny look, but as the man drove off, he gave them a wave.

Sam knew, from other incidents like this one, that not everybody wanted to live in a commune. Of course, Sam had seen the nearby town of Bisbee, Arizona, which wasn't a commune. He didn't think much of it. People only went there to buy things, and you needed money for that. It wasn't quite clear to Sam where money came from, except that he suspected some of it arrived in the mail from people's parents.

A couple of times Sam had seen kids his own age in town. He wanted to make friends, because all the other children in the commune were practically babies. But the boys in town jeered at him and held their noses. Dad said it was because they were afraid of anybody who was different from them. But Sam couldn't understand why they thought he smelled bad. Mom made him take a bath in the creek every day.

He could dimly remember a little bit about what life was like before they'd come to the commune. Mom and Dad had been in college. They'd lived in a little house near the campus, and it was surrounded by dozens of other houses just like it. Sam could remember playing on the brownish patches of grass that struggled to grow between the houses. It wasn't anything like the woods around the commune, where some places were dark and damp even on the hottest days of summer.

What Sam remembered most about those days were the parades. Dad had carried him on his shoulders and gave him a sign to wave. Mom still had it on the wall of their cabin: "War is Not Healthy for Children and Other Living Things."

Antiwar protest march

They joined a big crowd of people marching down the street chanting, "Stop the war!"

Sam remembered singing "We Shall Overcome" in the parade. They still sang it around the council fire at the commune. But it had seemed more exciting to Sam when he sang it sitting on Dad's shoulders.

Was that why the man from the electric company thought the people at the commune were strange? Maybe because the war was still going on and he thought they should be doing something to end it instead of living out here all by themselves?

The commune members argued about that among themselves. Every now and then they would hear about a big parade—they called it a demonstration—and some of the commune folk wanted to go join it. But it was usually far away, and Agatha always said no.

She claimed it would distract them from their main purpose. "We agreed to live together to advance our own spirituality," she said. "Anything that detracts from that is to be shunned."

Spirituality was a hard thing to understand. Sam liked spirituality when it meant going out in the forest and letting himself feel like he was part of everything. He liked to lie down and feel himself connecting with the ground, staring up at the treetops and watching the birds build their nests and know he belonged there too. He knew if he lay there long enough, the rain would wash down on him and turn him into earth. But not yet. He still had other things to do.

But when Agatha and some of the others talked about spirituality, Sam didn't like it so much. They made it sound like you had to give up a lot of other things to get it. Mom said he'd learn more when he was older, but so far he hadn't.

The last time they had a council meeting, one of the men said that fighting the war was spiritual too. "The government is killing people, and we should try to stop it," he said.

"It's not our government any longer," Agatha replied. "We agreed we came here to govern *ourselves.*"

Sam had looked at his father, hoping he'd speak up. Really, Sam wished they would all agree to go demonstrate against the war. It wasn't just that he thought the war was bad. It was that demonstrations were a lot more fun than hoeing weeds and canning fruit.

Sam's father didn't say anything that night, so as usual Agatha got her way. But a few days later Sam woke up to find his father was gone. Sam knew at once what it meant, because it had happened before.

"Your father went to find himself," Mother said. "Don't worry. He'll be back."

But Sam did worry. He didn't see why his father couldn't find himself without going somewhere else. Other people had left the commune and hadn't returned. Occasionally Agatha referred to them as "our weak sisters and brothers."

So Sam spent his days with one eye looking for his father, and the other on the mailbox. If *Popular Electronics* arrived when Dad wasn't here to defend it, Agatha might get rid of it.

The little cloud of dust way down the road was the first sign of the mail truck. It didn't stop at the commune every day, but today it did. Sam dropped his hoe and took off running.

The driver saw him and waved. He held the copy of *Popular Electronics* out the window of his little truck. As Sam reached for it, the driver said, "Wait a sec. I think I've got a letter for you too."

A letter? Maybe Dad had written them a letter? That wouldn't be like him, and Sam felt the back of his neck tingle. Maybe it was bad news. Maybe he wasn't coming back.

The mail driver peered at the envelope through the bottom of his bifocals. "Esther Aldrich," he read. "Common Sense Commune. Route 2, Box 280. You know her? She live here?"

Sam swallowed. "Yes. She's my mother."

"Well, make sure you give it to her, hear?"

"I will."

As Sam examined the letter, he was relieved to see the address wasn't in his father's handwriting. But that made him more curious. Who else would have sent Mom a letter?

He went looking for her, but when he found her, she was in the cookhouse baking bread with some of the other women. He didn't want to

EASY-TO-BUILD BURGLAR ALARM FOR APARTMENT USE

Popular Electronics

WORLD'S LARGEST-SELLING ELECTRONICS MAGAZINE

JULY 1976 / $1

MOBILE COMMUNICATIONS: CB vs. 2-METER FM

Microwave Ovens for the Home

CMOS Probe Extends Multimeter Use

Guide to Choosing TV & FM Antennas

Learning Electronic Theory With Hand Calculators

TEST REPORTS:
Nikko 7075 AM/FM Stereo Receiver
MXR Stereo Equalizer
SBE
Hick
Analog Multimeter

EXCLUSIVE!
Now You Can Build a HIGH-QUALITY INTELLIGENT TERMINAL

Esther

attract their attention, because he still had the copy of *Popular Electronics*.

So he hid that under his bed at their cabin and waited until after supper to give the letter to his mother.

She didn't seem to wonder why he hadn't given it to her sooner. Her eyes lit up when she saw the envelope, and she opened it quickly.

"It's from your grandfather," she said as she began to read it.

Sam didn't have to ask which grandfather. His father's parents didn't want to have anything to do with them. There had been a terrible fight when Sam's father told them he and Esther and Sam were going to live in a commune. They wanted Dad to work in his father's business and live in a big house like the one they owned.

No, this letter must be from Grandpa Jack Aldrich. He was one of the leaders of the people who were protesting the war. Sam remembered him as a tall, thin man—even taller than Sam's father—with hair so white it looked like he'd been standing in a snowstorm. Sam liked him, but sometimes Grandpa Jack forgot Sam's name and would call him David. That was the name of

Mom's brother, who had been killed in World War II.

Mom looked happy when she started reading the letter, but by the time she'd finished, her expression had changed. She frowned as she looked up at Sam. "He's coming to visit," she said. "Coming here!"

"Great!" Sam said, jumping to his feet. Grandpa was a scientist, and there were a lot of questions Sam wanted to ask him. Since Sam's father had left, there hadn't been anybody to explain what he read in *Popular Electronics*.

Mom shook her head. "He's going to want us to leave," she said.

"Leave? You mean leave the commune?"

"Yes."

Sam didn't say anything. As far as he was concerned, that would be the best thing that could happen. But then Dad would never find them again.

THREE

Signing Up

APRIL 14, 1970

LUCY WAS AMAZED AT HOW WELL DICK FIT IN WITH her family. Not that the Vivantis didn't welcome him. When Dick had explained what he wanted to do, Grandpop Rocco nodded. "You want to see what a family is like today, eh?" he said.

"Well," Dick replied, "in the finished movie we'll have more than one family. It would be kind of a cross section of America."

Rocco nodded. "Then I agree. We want to be part of it."

Surprisingly—to Lucy, at any rate—nobody else in the family disagreed. Her dad and Uncle Tony looked at each other warily when they heard the

33

news. Lucy knew what they were thinking: How would Dick's movie make them look?

Art and Mike, Uncle Tony's sons, had no such doubts. Each had a strong point of view, and they saw the movie as a way to express it. From the very first time Dick set up his cameras to film the Vivantis, Art and Mike carried on their heated argument about the war.

Lucy also noticed that her mom and Aunt Irene dressed better than usual for the dinner table. Aunt Irene spoke more distinctly, as if she were giving a speech. She even stopped using curse words when she told Art and Mike to stop arguing.

Worst of all, Lucy's younger sister Isabel decided she could become the star of the movie. She always managed to slip into a group that Dick

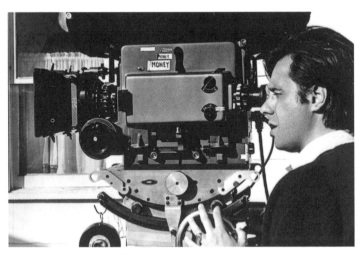

A 16mm movie camera

was filming, and often said something that sounded as if she'd been rehearsing it for days. Usually it was a statement about what kids today were thinking.

Grandmama Teresita was the only member of the family who didn't seem to like Dick bringing his cameras in. She always peered at the lens suspiciously and turned away when she drank her cup of espresso.

Lucy asked her one day, "Nonna, why don't you like being filmed?"

Grandmama put her finger to her nose. "This guy on the crutches, he's one of the Aldriches, isn't he?"

Lucy nodded. "A lot of them are in show business."

"A long time ago, I was pretty," said Nonna. "They didn't put me in their movies then. No, they wait till I'm practically seventy years old. That Nell, you know, she was always after your Grandpop."

"Nell? Nell Aldrich? No, you must be mistaken, Grandmama."

"Sure, and she still looks good. I would too if I had a lot of face-lifts and things done to me. Now they bring cameras to take my picture. Well, I just turn my back."

On the other hand, Aunt Gabriella seemed to enjoy the idea of being filmed almost as much as

Art and Mike did. Instead of staying cooped up in the kitchen, she now brought out the meals when they were ready and sat down with the rest of the family. If either Uncle Tony or Lucy's dad started to say anything about the quality of the food (that the other one had bought), Gabriella would poke them sharply and say, "Enough! Both of you know this is the best restaurant between New York and San Francisco. If either of you bought bad food, I wouldn't cook it. So stop yelling."

Dick didn't seem to mind the arguments. That was what he'd come here for, Lucy guessed. He wanted to see turmoil and Lucy had told him where to find it. But really she hadn't expected that he would just move right in. They gave him a spare room next to the pantry, and he didn't go to bed until everybody else was asleep.

Not only did the Vivantis welcome him, Lucy thought, but Dick never seemed to think *they* were strange. No matter what they did.

Art let his hair grow even longer and wore torn bell-bottom jeans with tie-dyed shirts. His brother Mike had a crew cut and usually wore a clean Oxford cloth shirt with a button-down collar. Nobody would have guessed they were brothers.

Art

Lucy's father often made jokes about Art looking like a girl. Personally, Lucy thought Art looked like a rock star, maybe a little like Jim Morrison. Uncle Tony didn't like the way his son Art looked either. But once Lucy's father started criticizing him, then of course Uncle Tony had to defend him.

Tony

"I looked worse than him back in the 1930s when I crossed the country in a freight car," said Uncle Tony.

"Don't start," warned Aunt Irene. Lucy felt the same way. He'd told the story of his trip to California dozens of times, and most of it nobody believed.

"You had an excuse, then," replied Lucy's father. "There weren't any places on the railroad line to get a haircut. We have barbers in Chicago."

"Hey, both of my boys graduated from college. That's more than you or I ever did."

"They only went to college to stay out of the draft. You and I enlisted to defend our country. These kids today—"

"You fought in World War II," Art interrupted. "That was a different kind of war. We were attacked and had to defend ourselves. The Vietnamese never did anything to us, and we have no business destroying their country."

"We're not fighting the Vietnamese," his brother Mike replied. "We're helping them to defend themselves from communism."

"That's ridiculous," Art shot back. "The Vietnamese were supposed to be allowed to vote for their government in 1956, but the United States wouldn't allow it."

"Because the Communists would have won."

"So? If they wanted to elect Communists—"

Lucy wanted to stick her fingers in her ears. She had heard all this a hundred times, and so had everybody else at the table. She remembered watching on TV the riots in Chicago during the Democratic National Convention of 1968. Art had

Democratic National Convention riots of 1968

actually gone down to Grant Park to join the anti-war demonstrators. Luckily he hadn't been arrested or beaten up by the police, although he did breathe a little tear gas.

But because of that, Art could say—as he always did at this point in the argument— "At least I have the courage to back up my convictions. I went and fought against the war machine."

This time, however, Mike surprised everybody by responding, "I know you did, so that's why I decided to enlist. I'm going to go fight communism."

That was one of the few times when nobody at the Vivanti dinner table had anything to say. There was a shocked silence. Even Art stared open-mouthed at his brother. He looked so stunned that Isabel giggled.

The boys' mother was the first to speak. "Enlist?" said Aunt Irene with a shriek. "Enlist in what?"

"The air force," Mike replied calmly. "If I waited to get drafted, I'd have to go in the army and I'd rather fly." From the time he was young, Mike had loved airplanes. He had dozens of model planes in his room, some on shelves, some hanging from the ceiling because he'd run out of space.

His father didn't care about that. "But you weren't going to be drafted," he said. "You had a high draft number. We were happy when the numbers were drawn because it meant you wouldn't have to go."

Mike shrugged. "Somebody has to go. Art's got a low number, and maybe if I enlist, he won't get drafted."

All eyes at the table turned to Art, who said, "Hey, it's not *my* fault. I didn't tell him to enlist. I said he should sign up for more courses at Loyola, like I did. That way, neither of us would get drafted."

"Sure," their father said encouragingly. "Go and do that, Mike. By June the war will probably be over anyway. Nixon promised he was going to get us out of Vietnam if he was elected."

"Oh, sure," said Art. "And look what he did. Increase the bombing. That's why they need people in the air force, Mike. But listen, you can still get out of it, even if you *have* enlisted. I know a guy who knows a doctor who will sign a paper saying you're mentally ill."

A loud bang silenced everybody again. Grandpop had brought his fist down hard on the table. It was the signal that he wanted to say something.

Grandpop looked hard at Mike. "You signed up already? The papers to join the air force? You put your name on them?"

"Yes, Grandpop," said Mike.

"Then it's settled," said Grandpop. He looked around the table. "He gave his word. When you sign something, you live up to it, or your word is trash. So he's going."

Mike's parents both started to say something and Rocco's fist came down again. Then he pointed to Art, saying, "And that means we no longer speak out against the war at this table."

Art looked as if words were filling up the inside of his head so fast that it might explode like a balloon. But Grandfather wagged his finger to keep them bottled up. "I'm not saying the war is a good thing," Grandpop continued. "War is never a good thing. I've seen enough to know that. And this war—" He stopped, as if he had caught himself from breaking the rule he had just set. "Anyway, while one of our family is in the war, we do not speak against it."

Art fumed, but he did it silently. He shot a glance at his brother, as if to say, *You just enlisted so you could win the argument.*

After dinner, as Dick changed the film in his camera, Lucy asked, "Does this mean you'll be moving somewhere else?"

He shook his head. "Not at all."

"When Grandpop says something," Lucy explained, "everybody has to do it. So . . . there aren't going to be any more arguments about the war."

"I didn't come just to see arguments," Dick told her. "I wanted to find out what this family thinks. You want to sit down for the camera now?"

"Me?"

"Sure."

"I haven't got anything to say."

"Everybody has something to say," he replied. "If you're not ready, I can interview your sister."

"Isabel? How much film have you got? She'll dance, sing, and do cartwheels for you. She loves to be the center of attention."

"How do you feel about that?"

She looked at him. "Is the camera running now?"

He smiled, and she figured it must be. Maybe it hadn't been a good idea to ask him to come here, she thought. She hoped later on her family wouldn't remember it had been *her* idea.

"Come on," said Dick. "I need your help."

"On what?"

"Questions. What do you think I should be asking people?"

"About the war?"

"That . . . and other things. What do you think of the war protesters?"

Lucy hesitated. She had listened to the arguments about the war ever since she could remember. Two years ago, her mother made Lucy and Isabel stay indoors for a week because she was afraid they would get hurt in the protests for the Democratic Convention.

On the other hand, Art was one of the protesters. Lucy couldn't say she was against him. He'd always been nice to her. But then, so had Mike. She couldn't really understand why he wanted to go to Vietnam and bomb people.

"I wish the war would stop," she said finally. "For everybody's sake."

The war didn't stop, but the arguments did. During the next two weeks, before Mike went off to training camp, nothing was said about the war at the dinner table. The day Mike left, his brother Art even shook his hand and wished him good luck. Aunt Irene cried. Grandmama gave him some *mustasole*, or hard cookies, that she had made as a surprise.

"When your grandparents came over on the ships from Italy, they brought these to eat," Grandmama told Mike. "They won't spoil no matter how long you keep them." Everybody laughed, because they all remembered how the *mustasole* caught in your teeth, like taffy. Nobody would eat them unless they were going on a long voyage.

"He won't need those," said Grandpop. "He's not going on a ship. He's going to fly. But he's got to go through training first. He might never get to Vietnam if Nixon keeps his promises."

Lucy saw Art grit his teeth to keep from saying something about Nixon.

Then Uncle Tony started to give Mike some final advice. "Do it the way we did on Okinawa in the Second World War. Keep your head down and don't volunteer for anything."

That was when Lucy's father just *had* to put his two cents worth in. "Don't listen to that kind of talk. Pick out where you want to be and aim for it. The important thing is—"

"Don't tell him what to do," Uncle Tony interrupted. "You can't even tell good olive oil from bad."

They were still arguing about that when the taxi came for Mike. Art tried to help him with his suitcase, but Mike wouldn't let him. They struggled with it a little, and Lucy dashed forward with a piece of paper. "I wrote something for you," she said, holding it out to Mike.

He gave her a big grin as he took it from her, even though Art got the suitcase away from him. "What's this?" Mike asked.

"Don't read it till you're on the plane," she whispered. "It's just a poem. And don't fight anymore with Art."

He winked at her. "OK. I can promise that because I won't be here for a long time."

She wished he hadn't said that. It seemed like bad luck.

FOUR

What's Learning Like?

GRANDFATHER LOOKED OLDER THAN SAM HAD remembered. The lines in his face seemed deeper and his eyes looked very tired. But there was no mistaking him when he came walking down the road that led to town. It was his long thin legs, which made him look like the shadow puppets one of the men at the commune made with sticks and a candle behind a sheet of paper.

When Sam ran to meet him, Grandfather tried to pick him up. But he couldn't. Instead, he sat down on the ground as if he were out of breath. To make him feel better, Sam sat next to him.

"Did you walk a long way, Grandfather?" asked Sam.

"I hitched rides most of the way," Grandfather said. "I only had to walk from the state highway, two or three miles. I guess I'm just tired out, that's all. Tired and old. But there's still work to be done," he added as if reminding himself. "Let's go meet the others."

Jack

Everybody in the commune knew who Grandfather was, and they held a feast of celebration for him. Andrew, the commune member everybody agreed was the best cook, had made soybean soup, peppers stuffed with pumpkin and sunflower seeds, and hummus, with onion and garlic. For dessert, Andrew made peanut butter and honey balls covered with walnuts. Everybody's fingers got sticky when they ate these, but then it was fun to lick them clean.

Many of the commune members asked Grandfather questions about what was happening in the world outside. They didn't have radios or TVs. The only time they learned any news was when somebody went into town and saw a newspaper or magazine.

Grandfather told them that the war was still going on. "Nixon has taken some of our troops out of Vietnam," he said, "but he increased the bombing and invaded Cambodia."

"Are the protests getting bigger?" someone asked.

"Yes, but Nixon is determined not to be influenced by them," Grandfather replied. "I'm afraid there is going to be more violence in this country. Some of the young people are impatient. They talk about overthrowing the government."

"Wow," somebody said. "That would be groovy."

Grandfather shook his head. "We need a government. If the government does something wrong, we should work to change it. But if you can overthrow it whenever you don't like what it's doing, then you'll eventually wind up with much less freedom than we have now."

There was silence. People looked at Agatha. "Why not do as we do?" she asked. "Live without the government."

He smiled. "I admire you for trying," he said.

Agatha seemed annoyed that he wouldn't argue with her. "We're not only trying," she said. "We're doing it."

"Are you going to join us?" one of the other commune members asked. "You're welcome to stay."

"For a little while," Grandfather replied. "I want to visit my daughter and grandson. But then . . ."

He trailed off and they understood. Grandfather had more important things to do, thought Sam.

When the feast ended, Grandfather went back to the cabin with Esther and Sam. He looked tired. "You can use my bed," Sam offered. "I don't mind sleeping on the floor."

But Grandfather had brought a sleeping bag and rolled it out. "I'm used to this," he said.

"Father," said Sam's mother, "Are you hiding from someone?"

"What makes you ask that?"

"The fact that you walked here. You have a car. Why not use it? And where's Mother?"

"Your mother is staying with friends. And you're right. I am hiding. Some government agency wants to keep track of me. It's easier to give them the slip if I travel alone."

"They're not going to arrest you, are they?"

He chuckled. "I hope not, for I haven't done anything but speak out against the war. For now, at least, we still have freedom of speech."

"So why—"

"Oh, I have a great many secrets locked in here," he said, tapping his forehead. "You remember the time we spent at Los Alamos during World War II? You were a great one for finding out secrets then. Well, the government is afraid I'll share some of those secrets with a country it regards as an enemy."

"You wouldn't do that," said Mother.

"Of course not," he said. "If it were in my power to make everyone in the world forget all those secrets we discovered at Los Alamos, I would do it."

Sam couldn't contain himself. "What secrets are those?" he asked.

Grandfather seemed a little embarrassed. "Atomic secrets," he replied quietly. "The secrets of killing more people at one time than anyone ever has before."

Sam caught his breath. "You mean the atomic bomb? You invented the atomic bomb?"

"Fortunately," said Grandfather, "the burden is not mine alone. It took many people to build the bomb, but yes, I was one."

"But you're totally against war," Sam said. That was the one thing he'd always known about Grandfather.

Grandfather nodded. "War seemed like a good thing in 1942, when Hitler was killing people in Europe. He would have killed your grandmother if we hadn't left Germany in time. I thought science could help defeat him. I was living in a little bubble. The science bubble."

Sam thought of the copy of *Popular Electronics* underneath his bed. Was that part of what Grandfather thought of as the science bubble?

"You don't think science is good?" Sam asked.

"Science isn't good or bad," said Grandfather. "It's what people use it for that can be good or bad. But there's only one way to use an atomic bomb."

Mother spoke up. "That's enough for tonight, Sam. Grandfather is probably tired. You should stay here for awhile, Father. You'll be safe here."

He shrugged. "I was safe for too long. That's why I didn't understand what I was doing."

They went to bed after that. Sam soon heard the sound of his grandfather's snores. It was comforting, because it was like having Dad back again. But what Grandfather had said filled Sam's head with a thousand questions.

In the morning, Mother went off early to recruit people for laundry duty. Sam went to the dining hall for breakfast and (against the rules) brought some food back for Grandfather.

He was awake when Sam returned, and the herb tea and scrambled eggs seemed to give him energy. "That field where I saw you yesterday," he said, "do you have to go back there today?"

"I'm supposed to," said Sam. "But nobody really checks. Unless you make a lot of trouble, you can pretty much do what you want around here."

"Why don't you give me a tour of the place, then?"

Proudly, Sam showed Grandfather the electric lines that his father had installed.

"Looks like a good job," said Grandfather. "Where is he now?"

"He went off to find himself, Mom says."

Grandfather snorted. "You know, Ed—your father—has some brains. Your mother does too. They could be doing something more—" He cut himself off, and looked at Sam as if he were afraid he'd said too much.

"That's OK," said Sam. "I'd like to get out of here too."

"You would? Don't they treat you well?"

"Oh, yeah," Sam replied. "That's not it. I kind of wish I could go to school. There's a lot I want to learn."

Grandfather nodded. "Don't your parents teach you?"

"Dad does when he's here. But they're both busy, you know."

"You can learn some things on your own," Grandfather said. "Do you have books here?"

"A few. Dad got a subscription to *Popular Electronics*. I was wondering if you could explain some of the diagrams to me."

"Well, my field was physics, not electrical engineering, but I'll give it a whirl."

They spent most of the morning leafing through the magazines that Sam had saved. Grandfather's explanations weren't quite as clear as Dad's. Grandfather wanted Sam to understand the reasons why certain things worked. Sam was more interested in how to put things together to make them work. But Grandfather eventually got around to that too. It just took a little longer.

Sam pointed to an advertisement in the magazine. "Do you think if we got that hi-fi kit, I could put it together?"

Grandfather smiled. "It's rather a big project. You'd need speakers too."

"Yeah . . . that's where the sound comes out, right? I guess they cost a lot of money."

Grandfather nodded.

"Do you have any money?" Sam asked.

"Enough," said Grandfather. "Scientists are paid well for what they do."

"Is there any book that would teach me all I need to know about science?" asked Sam.

"I don't think so," said Grandfather.

"Could you write one?"

Grandfather thought about it. "Even if I could, it wouldn't teach you everything you need. There are new things being discovered all the time. When I was your age, science was just starting to explore the atom. That's what I spent my life doing."

"What would you spend your life at if you were my age now?"

"Oh . . . there are so many new things. Lasers, perhaps. Or continue work on the transistor. Maybe computers. Someday it's possible they'll have more uses than merely making fast calculations. Or biology should be an interesting field . . . now that DNA has been discovered."

"What's DNA?"

"It's something like a road map within us that determines who we are."

"Really? I never heard of that." Sam wondered if Grandfather might be putting him on. "Are you sure?"

"As sure as a scientist can be. We're often wrong, don't forget."

"I didn't know that."

"You see, school is only a starting point. You've got to learn things on your own, and keep on learning throughout your life."

Sam was thinking that if Grandfather stayed, Sam wouldn't have to spend all his time doing things like hoeing weeds and making compost heaps. Grandfather was so popular that even Agatha couldn't stop him from doing what he wanted. "You could teach me if you stayed here, Grandfather," he said.

"Even if I stayed," Grandfather replied, "I don't have much time."

"Sure you do," Sam said. "They wouldn't make you work in the fields. At least not more than an hour or so a day."

"That's not the kind of time I mean," said Grandfather.

Sam was confused. What other kind of time was there?

"But you're right," Grandfather went on. "No matter how much time there is, it's better to make a start."

That night, Grandfather told Sam's mother what he was planning. "Sam has a good mind. He shouldn't be wasting it. I'll teach him what I can, but you ought to send him to school."

Mother looked at Sam as if he shouldn't be listening. "Schools are corrupt institutions," she said. "They fill children's minds with ignorance and fear."

"Esther," said Grandfather, "you went to school for twenty years. You were working on a doctorate. What kind of ignorance and fear did you learn?"

She frowned. "A lot. I just didn't want to bother you and Mother with it."

"You were a brilliant student," Grandfather responded. "As far as I could tell you enjoyed school, right to the end. We never understood why you chose to leave."

"Father," she said, "you of all people should have understood. Here you are, working to stop the war, when it was you who helped make war so dangerous."

Sam frowned. He could see that Grandfather was hurt by what Mother had said. "That may be," Grandfather responded after a few seconds, "but I still feel that ignorance is worse than the search for knowledge. You used to feel that way too. You were always curious about things, eager to learn. Why did you change? Why don't you want that for your son?"

Again Mother glanced at Sam. He wondered if he should leave the room. But this was too fascinating for him to go without being forced to.

"All that learning–school learning–didn't teach me what I really wanted to know," said Mother. "And one day I realized it never would. I had to look within myself."

Grandfather thought about that for so long that Sam thought he wasn't going to say anything. At last he spoke: "Have you found it yet?"

"No," said Mother. "But it's quieter here and I can listen better."

FIVE

A Demonstration

JUNE 14, 1970

THERE WAS NO DOUBT ABOUT IT. DINNER AT THE Vivantis wasn't the same since Mike left. Oh, Uncle Tony and his brother Leo—Lucy's father— still found things to argue about. And Grandmama found fault with the way the children (even those who were grown up) spoke or acted or dressed. The Vivantis couldn't stop arguing any more than they could stop eating. But silently they all worried about Mike. He had finished training and was now in Vietnam. His last letter said he was about to go on his first flight.

Actually, Mike's departure seemed to weigh heaviest on Art. Not only had he lost his favorite

57

person to argue with, but it also seemed wrong that Art was still there while his brother was off to war.

In fact, every time Art spoke out against the war now, it didn't sound as if his heart was in it anymore. Rocco only had to growl a little to make him stop.

Then one night, Art didn't sit down to dinner with everybody else. Well, you didn't have to, of course, thought Lucy. You could miss dinner if you had a good excuse. But it had to be a really good one—like if you were in a car wreck or stopped to rescue children from a burning orphanage.

As soon as they finished the soup, Rocco looked at Uncle Tony and said, "Where's Art?"

"I don't know," Tony mumbled. "Maybe he's got an evening class at the college."

"He graduated last June," said Rocco. "You don't remember that?"

"Maybe he signed up for more classes—it would be a good idea to get an advanced degree."

Rocco grunted. "More likely he's got a girl-friend. At least he could bring her home, introduce her. What do you think? Aren't we fancy enough?"

"I'll talk to him," said Uncle Tony.

But Art didn't get back until very late. He even missed his assigned turn as a waiter, which was also unusual. Long after the restaurant had closed, Lucy was lying awake, wondering how Dick's movie would show her family. Then she thought she heard somebody arguing downstairs. She sat up in bed to listen, but the only other sound was of doors slamming in the apartment where Uncle Tony's family lived.

In the morning, she could tell something had happened. Everybody was walking around all stiff and silent, as if they were waiting for someone to apologize. Breakfast was never as formal as dinner. The restaurant was closed, and if you wanted something to eat, you had to go into the kitchen to see what was on the stove or in the refrigerator.

Uncle Tony had already left for the fish market by the time Lucy came downstairs. Her father was putting on his coat, and gave her a look that meant, "Come over here, I want to talk to you."

He turned and spoke in a low voice. "Don't say anything about Art, hear me?"

"Art?" she said. "What happened to him?" Maybe he was in a car accident and was in the hospital or worse.

"He came home to get some clothes and went somewhere else to stay. So just keep your trap shut." Waving a finger of warning at her, he left.

Somewhere else? Keeping her mouth shut was going to be almost impossible, because Lucy had a million questions. She filled a plate with some asparagus frittata, poured herself some orange juice, and sat down at one of the long kitchen worktables.

Aunt Irene, Art's mother, looked as if she'd been crying, and Lucy's mother was talking softly to her. It seemed like the kind of conversation that would abruptly stop if Lucy slipped over to listen.

In fact, Grandmama came up to her just then and said, "You're going to be late for school."

"It's Saturday," said Lucy.

Grandmama sniffed as if somebody had played a trick on her. "Well, it's a beautiful day. Go out and play."

Lucy took her plate, which was still half full, and went into the dining room. She always liked sitting out here when it was empty. Grandpa had hung photographs on the wall, showing parties and dinners over the years. Lucy liked to imagine she could hear the echoes of people who had enjoyed themselves in this room.

But it wasn't quite empty. Dick was changing the film in one of his cameras. "Have they found Art yet?" he asked.

"You know as much as I do," Lucy told him. "Probably more. Did they tell you to get out of the kitchen?"

He nodded, smiling. "But don't tell anybody," he said. "I've got a camera still running in there."

She giggled in spite of herself. What would Mother and Grandmama and Aunt Irene say if they found out?

"What are you doing with all this film?" she asked.

"Well, it has to be edited eventually," Dick told her. "That's really work. Out of a couple hundred reels of film, I've got to find the best parts and fit them together so they make sense."

"Make sense to who?"

"To an audience."

"So you decide what's important to show and what's not?"

"You could say that," he said. "But I'm going to try to make it true to the family."

"When will you be finished?"

"I don't know," he replied. "I think it should have an ending, and it doesn't seem to me that there is one yet."

"Maybe with families . . . there's never an ending. As long as there are children to carry the story on."

"There are always little endings," Dick replied. "Even though the story of the family might continue."

Lucy thought about this. "Does that mean someone has to die before a story ends?"

"I hope not," he said, snapping the camera shut. "That would make every story pretty sad, wouldn't it?" He stood up and tried to bring the movie camera to eye level. He had a little trouble doing that and balancing on his crutches at the same time.

"Where's the tripod?" Lucy asked. Usually Dick rested the camera on a tripod and just let it run.

"I won't be able to use it today," he said. "I'm going to be moving around while I shoot."

"What are you going to film?"

"I thought I'd look for Art," he said.

Lucy was surprised. "Where will you look? He could be anywhere."

"He *could* be," said Dick, "But I have a little idea where." He picked up a copy of the *Chicago Tribune* and pointed to a headline:

"I have a feeling that Art might be somewhere in the middle of this," said Dick.

Lucy nodded. Of course he would. "I could help you," she said. "You'll need somebody to carry the camera."

It wasn't hard to find the protest demonstration. After they took the El train to the Loop, all they had to do was follow the lines of police. As they walked closer to Grant Park, they could hear the sounds of chanting, drumbeats, and singing. They weren't happy sounds, Lucy thought. They were angry sounds, as if the people making them were challenging others to try and stop them.

With Lucy carrying the camera, Dick had no trouble moving along the crowded sidewalks. In fact, Lucy had to struggle to keep up with him. Finally he stopped and pointed toward a hill. "Let's go up there," he said. "We'll have a good view of everything that's going on."

After they climbed it, Lucy saw that he was right. Down below, a small group of demonstrators were waving signs and singing. They were surrounded by a ring of blue-uniformed policemen. Beyond them were crowds of onlookers who were just curious about what was going on.

It was funny in a way, thought Lucy. Most of the demonstrators looked like Art—the boys with long hair and colorful clothing, the girls wearing long granny dresses or jeans, with flowers in their hair. Some of them waved flags, either American or North Vietnamese.

But compared with the policemen and onlookers, there were really just a tiny number of demonstrators. What was funny was that they could attract so many other people to guard them or watch them. They didn't look very dangerous. Lucy wondered why everybody seemed so afraid of them. In school, she had learned you were allowed freedom of speech. Art had always said the antiwar demonstrators were only expressing that right.

"There he is," said Dick, pointing to the place where the demonstrators stood. Lucy looked and saw him too. Art was right in the midst of them, wearing a shirt with red stripes that looked as if it had been made out of a flag. Even from this distance, Lucy could see he was singing and looked happier than she'd seen him in weeks.

Dick took the camera from her and shot some film. "I haven't got a telephoto lens," he said. "I'd like to get a close view of him, but there are too many people in the way."

Lucy saw what he meant. Even if they could push their way through the crowd of spectators, the police would probably stop them from getting any closer.

Then she spotted someone else she knew. She'd seen him many times in the restaurant. He was a friend of Grandpop's.

"See that policeman over there?" she asked Dick. "The one who's ordering the others around?"

Dick nodded.

"He's . . ." Lucy tried to think. "Reilly. That's his name. Grandpop calls him Mike, but he's Captain Reilly. If we tell him what we want, maybe he'll let us go through."

"It's worth a try," said Dick.

Lucy took the camera and they made their way down the hill and through the crowd. As they got closer, the noise grew louder and scarier. She could hear the demonstrators shouting and waving their banners in the policemen's faces. It was like they were daring the police to do something about it.

Lucy remembered all the violence that had broken out at the Democratic Convention two years ago. *That* had caused a lot of arguments at the Vivanti dinner table. Art said the police were to blame. Grandpa Rocco didn't want to hear it, but Lucy could see the television pictures of policemen beating up demonstrators had bothered him.

Now here was Art right in the middle of another protest. Lucy could see that the police were angry, looking at the demonstrators as if they'd like to go after them again. But after all the bad publicity they'd gotten, they had to hold back.

Probably all they would have to do was step out of the way and the spectators would do the job. A lot of them were tough-looking construction workers, who were yelling back at the demonstrators. Calling them names like, "Traitors! Commies!" and even worse things. Even some men in business suits and ties, who were on their lunch hour, seemed angry. The demonstrators weren't winning anybody over to their side, Lucy thought.

Finally she and Dick got close to Captain Reilly, and Lucy waved to catch his attention. For a moment she thought he wasn't going to recognize her. But then his face lit up and he walked over. "Lucy, isn't it?" he said. "Lucy Vivanti, Rocco's granddaughter—what are you doing in the middle of all this? Go home before you get hurt."

"Captain Reilly," she said quickly, as if she hadn't heard him, "this is Dick Aldrich. He's staying with our family and making a movie. Could you help us to get closer to the demonstration?"

The burly police officer gave Dick a frown. "Neither of you ought to be here," he said. "And the Chicago police, you know, aren't too fond of TV reporters and their cameras, coming here to make us look bad."

"That's not what I'm doing," said Dick. "I'm making a film about families. The Vivantis have given me permission to film them."

"So what are you doing here?" Captain Reilly asked.

"One of the Vivantis is up there," Dick said, pointing to the demonstrators.

Captain Reilly looked over his shoulder in surprise, then back at Dick. "Oh, must be that Artie, Tony's younger son. Well, a bad apple in every barrel, eh? I'm sure Rocco doesn't want *him* in the movie. So why don't you just turn around and go back, instead of putting this little girl in danger. And yourself," he said, looking at Dick's crutches. "If there's any trouble, you could be run right over."

"It was my idea," said Lucy. "And I'm not a little girl. I'm twelve."

Captain Reilly motioned to a younger policeman standing nearby. He pointed to Lucy and Dick and said, "Escort these two out of harm's way, Eddie."

"You can't make me leave," said Dick. "This is a public park."

Captain Reilly gave him a hard look. "Did you bring this girl here?"

Dick glanced at Lucy. "Well . . . yes," he said.

"Then I'll arrest you for endangering a minor unless you take her away."

Lucy was incensed. "I wanted to come here," she protested. "He didn't endanger me."

Captain Reilly ignored her. "Make up your mind," he told Dick.

So they let the younger policeman take them back out to the edge of the crowd. It made Lucy feel humiliated. "That wasn't fair," she said. "I'm going to tell Grandpa about this."

"We can still film the demonstration," Dick said. "I have a feeling something is going to happen."

"Why?" asked Lucy as they walked back up the hill they had stood on earlier.

"Because that police officer was so eager to get us out of there," he said. "Bring the camera over here." They quickly set up the tripod and Dick looked through the viewfinder, focusing on the demonstration below.

He was just in time, for a scuffle broke out on the edge of the crowd of protesters. Though Lucy looked closely, she wasn't able to see what caused it. But she saw demonstrators and police pushing each other angrily, as a loud roar arose from both sides.

Then she saw Artie, unmistakable in his red-striped shirt. He was trying to get to where the fighting had begun. She couldn't tell whether he wanted to join it or stop it.

Then a policeman stepped up and raised his billy club. He looked like he was going to knock Art's brains out. Lucy screamed, and even though Art couldn't possibly have heard her, he sensed what was happening and ducked out of the way just in time. The policeman was thrown off balance when his blow failed to hit its target. He stumbled forward and then fell.

With a cry of triumph, other protesters standing nearby leaped toward the spot. It looked like they were going to stomp the policeman. Then a wall of police rushed forward to meet them. Now everybody on both sides joined the fighting. To Lucy, it seemed like a crowd of crazy people, hitting each other for no reason.

She scanned the mob, trying to see what had happened to Art. But the red-striped flag shirt had disappeared. All she could see were police and demonstrators striking out at each other. Their shouts and cries carried up the hill, and she could hear the pent-up anger. She wrapped her arms around herself and wished she hadn't come to see this.

The Sweat Lodge

JUNE 1970

SAM'S GRANDFATHER DECIDED TO TAKE PART IN the commune's work. So Sam found him a hoe and took him to the vegetable fields. Sam was disappointed because he would much rather have Grandfather teach him science.

As it turned out, Grandfather didn't last very long in the fields. His hands got blistered from the hoe and when he stubbornly kept working, the blisters burst. Sam's mother noticed them at dinner. "What have you been doing?" she asked.

Grandfather tried to put his hands under the table, but Mother made him go to LuAnn, the commune's healer. She wrapped his blisters with a poultice of herbs.

Well, that meant he couldn't hoe any longer, but the next day he went along with Sam anyway.

"You know those things you were talking about?" Sam asked.

"What things?"

"Science things—lasers and transistors. Maybe you could teach me about them now."

Grandfather laughed, and then coughed as if it hurt him to laugh. "All right. I can see that you're determined."

At first Grandfather just walked behind Sam and talked. He told Sam whatever came into his head. "Do you know why pulling up the weeds helps the tomatoes and beans?"

"I guess it gives them more room to grow."

"That's not quite the reason. The weeds compete with the vegetables for water and nutrients in the soil. But I see even where you've eliminated the weeds, your vegetables aren't growing well."

Sam looked at the part of the field he'd already hoed. What Grandfather said was true. Even though he'd carried buckets of water to the plants day after day, they looked puny and spindly.

"I don't know what's wrong with them," he said.

"It's this," Grandfather said, reaching down and picking up a handful of the soil. "Not enough nutrients in it. You need fertilizer."

"That's what Dad said," Sam replied. "But the others say fertilizer isn't natural. They're making compost heaps to put on the soil."

"That should help," said Grandfather. "Take the weeds you dig up and add them to the compost."

"I don't know," Sam said. "Somebody in the commune said weeds have bad spirits and will ruin the compost."

"Nonsense," said Grandfather. "Do you know what a compost heap is?"

Sam shook his head. "As far as I can see, it's just a pile of garbage. Scraps left over from meals, sawdust . . . people put anything in it that will turn into compost."

"Anything that will rot," said Grandfather. "Organic matter. Things that grew or were made from things that grew. Do you know why it rots?"

Sam thought about it. "Because it's dead?"

"Dead, yes, but the bacteria—tiny living organisms in the soil, in the air—they absorb the organic material and turn it into humus."

Sam stopped to consider this. "You mean germs?"

"Germs are harmful bacteria. The vast majority of bacteria are helpful. You couldn't survive without them."

They went on talking like that, and at the end of the day Sam wished he had a microscope so he could see some of the bacteria Grandfather was talking about. Because he was thinking about that, Sam didn't notice how tired Grandfather looked. But Sam's mother did right away.

"You were supposed to rest, Father," she said when they arrived at the cottage. "Sam, you know your grandfather isn't supposed to be working. He isn't used to the sun."

"I'll be fine," said Grandfather.

"Go inside," said Mother. "I'll go get some herbs from LuAnn and make you a tea. Lie down and rest. And Sam . . . see to it that he does."

After she'd gone, Sam took a good look and saw that all the color had drained from Grandfather's face. His hands were shaking too. "I'm sorry," said Sam. "I should have quit work earlier."

"What for?" replied Grandfather. "We had a good day together, didn't we? At my age, the good days don't come very often."

"Yeah, we did," Sam admitted. "I learned a lot. If you stayed here a year . . ."

"It won't be that long," Grandfather said. "I wish we could have had more days. But I can give you something you might be able to use." He reached into his pocket. Sam half expected him to come out with money, but instead he produced a small gold pen and a brown leather notebook that looked as if Grandfather had carried it for a long time.

"Do you have a piece of paper?" Grandfather asked.

Sam found a pad on Dad's worktable.

Grandfather copied something from the notebook. His writing was shaky, but Sam could see he'd written some numbers. "That's a phone number for Nell Aldrich," said Grandfather. "She's your . . . well, you're related. If you need anything, call her."

"Really?" said Sam. "Does Mother know her?"

"She was great friends with Nell's sister Peggy. But that doesn't matter. Tell Nell you're my grandson and she'll help you."

"What should I ask her for?"

Grandfather smiled. "That's up to you. But remember the old saying—be careful what you ask for. You might get it. Put that paper away now. Your mother will be back soon."

Sam realized it was kind of a secret between him and Grandfather. For some reason, Mother must not like Nell Aldrich. He tucked the paper into the back pocket of his jeans.

The tea seemed to have a soothing effect. After drinking it, Grandfather fell asleep in a chair. "Maybe we should put him to bed," Sam suggested. But mother said he could rest just as well in the chair.

In the morning, Sam was up first. He had thought of a question he wanted to ask Grandfather. The old man was still sitting upright, with his head resting against the back of the chair. But he looked different—maybe not as old as he had last night.

For a moment, Sam thought he might be dead. But then he realized that Grandfather's chest was still moving up and down slightly as he breathed.

Sam touched Grandfather's arm, but he didn't wake up. Soon Mother came out to the front room. She tried to wake him too, without success. "I think I'll go and find LuAnn," she said. "She'll know what to do."

Sam wasn't so confident in LuAnn's skill. Sometimes she made teas that caused people to act crazy. He looked into the cup next to Grandfather's chair. It was half full. Maybe it was good that he hadn't drunk all of it.

Mother returned with LuAnn, who picked up Grandfather's hand and looked at his fingernails. Then she opened one of his eyelids with her thumb and peered carefully at him. "I think we should take him to the sweat lodge," she said.

Sam tried to tell Mother that wasn't a good idea, but she wouldn't listen to him. At LuAnn's direction, two of the men came and carried Grandfather away. The sweat lodge was a canvas-covered frame like an Indian tepee. They built a fire outside and heated stones in it. Then the stones were brought inside the lodge on shovels. There,

LuAnn would spread herbs on the hot stones and pour water over them. The steam that filled the lodge was supposed to cure illness. To Sam, it had always been just a bad-smelling place. He was glad he'd never been sick enough to have to go there.

This time, he went to see if there was any way he could help Grandfather. But as word spread that he was sick, the other commune members gathered. Some of them went inside the sweat lodge to see him, and when LuAnn brought the heated stones, the commune members began to chant.

It wasn't words that they chanted. It was sounds like a long humming noise. Those inside the lodge took one another's hands, formed a circle around Grandfather, and began to dance. Sam was caught up in it, and felt helpless. The sounds grew louder. Some people were imitating birds.

If they expected this would help Grandfather, it didn't work. He just lay motionless on the blanket that had been spread on the ground. Every now and then someone would go out to replenish the supply of hot rocks.

Steam filled the lodge, carrying an odor that was both sharp and sweet. The dancing and chanting, the hot, moist air—it all started to make Sam feel dizzy. He wasn't the only one. People started to drop out of the circle, collapsing on the ground, gasping for breath. Finally Sam did too, and heard someone say, "This is good. Our energy will flow into him, make him strong."

Sam wondered if that were true. Was LuAnn's kind of healing what Grandfather wanted? More important, would it help him? It was impossible to tell. He crawled over and knelt beside Grandfather, reaching to take his hand. It was warm.

LuAnn entered the door of the lodge again, smiling as if she'd made a discovery. She carried a bowl, and when Sam saw what was inside, he cringed.

It held grayish-green pieces of cactus. Not just any kind of cactus, but the kind that made people see things that weren't really there. Twice before, Sam could remember LuAnn bringing out this cactus. Once, in the spring, when they had planted the seed for that year's crops. She said that this would help them get in touch with the spirits, who would ensure a good harvest. And before that, a long time ago, when the commune had started.

Sam hadn't taken any of the cactus then. His dad wouldn't let him. But everybody who did eat some began to act crazy. Or maybe it only seemed crazy if you hadn't eaten the cactus.

Now LuAnn was going from person to person, offering them the bowl. Soothingly she explained that they had to call on the spirits again to help their elder brother, Jack Aldrich.

When the bowl came to him, Sam looked down into it. He was afraid. Afraid that if he ate a piece, he would go crazy. But also afraid that if he didn't, the spirits would let Grandfather die.

He reached out and took one. LuAnn smiled and moved on.

Sam kept the cactus piece in his hand. It felt hard and rough, like a stone. As he watched, others put the pieces into their mouths. It didn't take long for something to happen. Pretty soon people began to chant again. Only this time, it wasn't all in unison. They called out whatever came into their minds—or the names of whatever they were seeing.

It was scary, not only because Sam couldn't see what the others were seeing, but because their voices were loud and strange. He was glad that Grandfather still lay peacefully sleeping.

All of a sudden someone came and sat in front of Sam, blocking his view.

His eyes focused, and he saw it was his mother. She was looking at him strangely. He knew at once that she'd eaten the cactus. Maybe he should try to get her out of here.

"David?" Her eyes looked deeply into his, and he was afraid of what he saw. "David," she said again. "I'm glad you're here. Father is ill. You have to help him."

Sam shook his head. "I'm not David," he said. "I'm Sam."

He knew David was Mother's older brother, and that he'd been killed in World War II. Mother still had an old photograph of him. She kept it in a book with some tattered newspaper clippings and a letter. Sam had found it once, but couldn't read the letter. It was written in some kind of code.

Now, Mother gripped Sam's arms and said, "You shouldn't have gone away, David. We still needed you. You could have told me about what you were doing–all the secrets."

Sam twisted away from her. She wasn't as strong as he thought. The cactus had made her move slowly and clumsily.

He got to his feet, feeling a little dizzy. There wasn't anything more he could do here, unless he wanted to eat the cactus and go crazy like everyone else. But he had made up his mind. He tossed the piece of cactus on the ground.

Stumbling, he made his way toward the door of the sweat lodge. He had to dodge a man who was dancing with someone nobody else could see.

Outside the air was so clean that Sam could hardly breathe it at first. Gradually, he rid his lungs of the smells of the lodge. He still felt shaky, but better than he had inside.

No one else was around. Sam knew what he had to do. He walked toward the desert, where his father had gone to find himself. Now Sam had to find him.

SEVEN

The Trial

"IT WAS JUST LUCK," LUCY SAID. "WE HADN'T PICKED that spot out on purpose. The policeman made us go there. We really wanted to get closer to the demonstration."

"It was a good thing you didn't," said Lorraine. She jotted some notes down on her yellow legal pad. "A lot of people who were near the fighting got hurt."

Lucy looked around. She'd never been in a lawyer's office before. But she didn't think very many lawyers had posters of cartoon characters on their walls. Her father had told her that Lorraine's brother was the person who had drawn The

no. 341
October

THE MASKED CRUSADER

Masked Crusader when it was still a comic book. That was before there was a Masked Crusader cartoon show on TV on Saturday mornings.

Of course, Lucy had seen Lorraine and her family in the restaurant. And she knew Lorraine's niece and nephew were part of a golden-oldie rock group years ago. But Lucy hadn't made the connection with Marcus Dixon, who was supposed to be so weird he never gave interviews or let himself be photographed.

"Um . . . excuse me?" She realized that while she was looking at the drawings, Lorraine had asked her a question.

Lorraine smiled. "I see you're interested in my brother's drawings. I'll see if I can get him to make one for you."

"Really?" Lucy was thinking what the kids at school would say.

"But right now," Lorraine went on, "we've got to talk about what happened at the park. It's important."

Lucy nodded. She knew it was. Her cousin Art had been arrested along with about twenty other protesters. They were accused of starting a riot, and Lorraine was going to defend them at the trial.

The protesters said they were only defending themselves. They claimed the police started the fight. The police insisted that the protesters had come there to cause a disturbance and that one of them set off the fighting.

The film Dick took that day might have shown which side was right. But Dick had refused to give up the film—something that made just about everybody mad at him.

Lucy remembered the night that the Vivantis stopped arguing among themselves and began to argue with Dick. He turned out to be a lot tougher than he looked.

"What's the film show?" Uncle Tony asked. "That's all we want to know. If it's proof Art had nothing to do with the fight, then you've got to let us have it."

"I wasn't shooting a movie so that it could be used in a trial," Dick said. "I need people to trust me, or nobody will ever let me film them."

Uncle Tony's face kept getting redder. "Well, we trusted you and let you film us," he said. "And now we need you to show that film. I can't understand what's the matter with you."

Aunt Irene broke in. She all but screamed in Dick's face. "My son is gonna go to jail! And you could keep him out of there." She turned to

Grandpop. "Aren't you going to tell him?" she asked. "It was you who said he could come here and move in with us."

Grandpop spread his hands. "He said he wanted to make a movie, is all. And Nell told me he's a good boy, like her son almost."

"Nell!" That was Grandmama, who for some reason had never liked Nell Aldrich. "She's nothing but trouble for us."

Grandpop shook his head. "Teresita," he said, "Nell took Tony into her home when he ran away, long ago. So we owed her a favor."

"It was your fault Tony ran away," Grandmama told Grandpop. "If you hadn't—"

And they were off again, arguing among themselves.

Right after that, Dick decided to move out. Lucy sneaked upstairs when she heard the news. She found Dick packing his clothes.

"Does this mean the movie is finished?" she asked.

He smiled. "Not a good way to end it, is it?"

"No, I mean what's going to happen to Art? Or to Mike? And now . . . you're part of the story because you won't give up the film. I don't know how you can just leave."

"I'm just getting out of the way for a while. The story will go on without me, and I'll be back for the ending."

"Why won't you let them have the film?" Lucy asked. "Then you could stay." She hesitated, wondering if she should say what she was thinking. "It's going to be boring without you. Everybody's just going to be arguing all the time."

"You shouldn't let that bother you," he said. "I think they like to argue."

She laughed, even though she didn't want to. "But why won't you? I mean, the film just shows what really happened."

"Believe me," he said. "Even if I did, it still wouldn't make everybody happy."

When Lucy thought about that later, she realized what it must mean. Dick thought the film showed the protesters started the fighting.

He snapped his traveling bag shut, and Lucy helped him carry it downstairs. His film equipment was already there, all boxed up. "I can handle it from here," Dick said. "A couple of men are coming with a truck."

"Will we see you again?" She was sad to think she might not.

"You can count on it," he said. He shook her hand. "You were a great help, Lucy," he said. "When the film is finished, you and your family will be the first ones to see it."

That same night, Uncle Tony suddenly realized something. He snapped his fingers and pointed at

Lucy. She had a sinking feeling in her stomach. "You were there with Dick at the park, right? When he made the movie?"

She nodded.

"So you can go to court and testify that Art had nothing to do with the riot."

At first, Lucy's parents hadn't liked the idea. But after another family fight, they decided it was all right. "Look," said Lucy's mother, "you just have to tell the truth."

"I'm not sure it *is* the truth," said Lucy.

"You're not saying Art had anything to do with starting the fight, are you?" asked Aunt Irene. "Because all he did was hang out with the wrong people."

Lucy looked at her, then at Uncle Tony. They would really be angry if she didn't help get Art out of jail. And Lucy didn't want any more arguments. So she agreed.

In the lawyer's office, however, Lorraine sensed Lucy's hesitation. "Are you worried about testifying?" Lorraine asked.

"A little," Lucy admitted.

"That's why we are going over the testimony now," said Lorraine.

"To make sure I say the right thing to get Art off?"

"No," said Lorraine. "Not if that's not the truth. What I do want is to know just what you saw in the park. Do you think you remember?"

Lucy thought for a while and then nodded. "Yes, I do remember."

"Good. Then tell me the full story, and I'll break it down into questions and answers in the courtroom."

Lucy went through the story of what she had seen that day. She didn't admit she hadn't seen the actual beginning of the fighting. After all, she had seen the policeman hit the demonstrator with his club. That was what was important—that and getting Art out of jail. Lorraine just nodded and didn't interrupt her.

When Lucy finished, Lorraine said, "One thing I'm not sure about. You don't seem to be sure of yourself when you describe how the fighting began."

Lucy hung her head. "The truth is," she said, "I didn't really see how it began. But my family wants me to say . . . you know, that the police started it."

"Well, I don't," Lorraine replied. "Not if you don't believe that."

"But then it won't help if I testify."

Lorraine shook her head. "I'll ask you questions that you can answer. Let me handle that. But remember, the prosecutor—the other lawyer—is going to try to trip you up. Understand? He'll ask you questions, hoping you'll change your story a little. Then he can say you're making the whole thing up."

"But I'm not, really," said Lucy. "That's what I saw."

Lorraine nodded. "I just want you to know there will be a lot of pressure on you."

Lorraine didn't know how much, really. In the days leading up to the trial, all Lucy could think about was her testimony. She went over and over it in her head. In school, she couldn't concentrate on anything the teacher said. At home, she lost her appetite so that everybody thought she must be coming down with something. Grandmama even made some of her famous pasta and bean soup that nobody could resist. "Everybody's counting on you, Lucy," said Grandmama as she pushed the bowl toward her. "You can't get sick."

All the attention only made Lucy feel more nervous and upset. She kept thinking that in the middle of her testimony, Dick would suddenly appear in the courtroom with his film. And it would show that she was lying.

On the day of the trial, everybody in the family wanted to go. Except Aunt Gabriella. "If I go, we'll have to close the restaurant," she said.

"Nobody could be in charge of the kitchen except a Vivanti." They agreed.

There were so many of them they had to go in two cars. Lucy sat in the backseat, with Isabel beside her jabbering about how lucky Lucy was. "Everybody will be looking at you," Isabel said. "You'll be the star witness, just like on the *Perry Mason* show." Lucy wondered what would happen if she threw up on Isabel.

When they arrived at the courthouse, Lucy had to be separated from the rest of the family. They all went to the visitor's section of the courtroom, but she had to stay in a special room for witnesses. Lorraine had told her this would happen, but it still made Lucy feel as if she were the one going to jail. All she could do was sit there and wonder what was going on at the trial. She kept repeating the words that she had practiced saying in Lorraine's office.

Finally the bailiff came to bring her into the courtroom. They entered through a side door that brought them right out in the front. As Lucy sat down in the witness chair, she could feel everybody's eyes on her. She looked over and saw Art and some of his friends sitting at a table with Lorraine. Art gave her a little smile.

Farther back, in the spectator section, she saw her family. Everybody looked serious except Isabel, who waved gaily at her.

The bailiff held out a Bible and Lucy put her hand on it. She swore to tell the truth, feeling that maybe she was going to hell after testifying. All she really had to say was, "I do," but it came out so quietly that the judge told her, "You'll have to speak a little louder, young lady."

She repeated, "I do," maybe too loudly this time, because some people in the spectator section laughed. The judge, who had a round reddish face, looked down at her and said, "You understand what the oath means?"

Feeling miserable, she nodded. "You have to say yes or no when you're asked a question," the judge told her. "So the stenographer can record it."

"Yes," she said.

"Don't be afraid," the judge added. "Just tell the truth about what you saw." *Right*, thought Lucy, *and then my family will kill me.*

Then Lorraine stood and began to ask Lucy questions they had practiced. Lucy had to describe where she had been standing in the park and how close it was to the demonstration.

Now came the important part: "While you were looking at the demonstration," asked Lorraine, "did you see fighting between the police and the demonstrators?"

Lucy blinked. Well, she could answer that truthfully. "Yes," she said.

"What was the first sign of fighting that you saw?"

"A policeman raised his club to hit one of the demonstrators."

"You're certain of that?"

"Oh, yes. He was wearing a uniform."

"Who was?"

"Oh. The policeman. That's why I could see him."

Lorraine looked at her notes, and then continued. "Did you see any reason for the policeman to hit the demonstrator?"

"No."

"What happened then?"

"The demonstrator ducked out of the way and pushed the policeman. He was only trying to defend himself."

"Do you see the demonstrator here today?"

"Yes." Lucy pointed to Art. "He's the second person from the left at that table."

After a few more questions about what else Lucy saw, Lorraine finished. Lucy wished it was all over now, but the prosecutor stood up. He reminded her of one of the priests in their church, Father Roman. He was the priest nobody wanted to go to confession to, because he'd scold you and give you a long penance.

"What were you doing in the park that day?" the prosecutor asked.

"I was with a man who was making a movie."

"Did he take pictures of the demonstration?"

"Yes."

"And where is he now?"

"Objection!" That was Lorraine, who said the question didn't have anything to do with the case. She and the prosecutor argued in front of the judge for a while. Finally the judge told the prosecutor to ask something else.

He turned back to Lucy. "Did you talk with a policeman in the park that day?"

"Yes."

"Did he order you to leave the park?"

Lorraine objected before Lucy could answer. Lucy was annoyed, because she was going to say no, the policeman just told them to get out of the way.

The judge stopped the questions about the police, so the prosecutor tried another tack. He didn't look discouraged. Lucy wondered if she would have to sit there all day.

"The demonstrator you identified before," the prosecutor began. "Are you related to him?" He sure knew a lot.

Lorraine objected again, but this time the judge overruled her.

So Lucy said, "Yes, he's my cousin."

"Your cousin." The prosecutor said it as if Lucy had just admitted starting the riot herself. He turned and looked at the jury, letting them know that something important was going on. He faced Lucy again and asked, "In fact you live in the same building with his family, isn't that true?"

"Well, with his family," said Lucy. "But he moved out."

"So you certainly want to see your close cousin get out of jail, don't you?"

Another objection. Lucy didn't have to answer.

Now the prosecutor surprised Lucy. "What do you think about the war?" he asked her.

"The war?"

"Yes, the Vietnam War. Do you think—"

"Ob-jec-tion!" Lorraine interrupted very loudly this time.

When the lawyers came before the judge, Lucy turned in her seat. "Judge," she said, then caught herself. "Your honor, I mean. I'd really like to answer that question."

"No, she wouldn't," said Lorraine.

"I agree," the judge said. "You don't have to answer it."

"But can I anyway?" Lucy asked. "I think it's important."

"The jury doesn't need to know what you think of the war," the judge told her.

"But I'm supposed to tell the whole truth, right?" asked Lucy. "Isn't that what the oath means?"

The judge smiled. Lucy hadn't known he could smile. "Very well. You may speak. But if this turns out to be an antiwar speech, I'll have to stop you."

Before Lorraine went back to her table, she gave Lucy a look that said she didn't like this.

Lucy took a deep breath. Maybe she shouldn't say anything. Everybody would be mad at her if she said something dumb. She was lucky to get this far without having to lie. But for a long time this had been building up inside her, and it seemed like the right time to get it out.

"I've heard all about the war," she began. "Every night at dinner. For years." She looked over at the jury, because a couple of them had laughed softly. "You see," Lucy went on, "I have another cousin. He's in the air force. He's in favor of the war. But the thing is . . . it's making us fight. My family argues about it all the time. And what happened in the park . . . that was just a bigger fight."

She paused again, thinking of the right words, because she wanted to say this just right. "It didn't really matter who started the fight. The demonstrators were angry. The police were angry. It's true, one of them told me to get away, because he was a friend of my Grandpop's. And all I was doing was watching. But he knew there would be a fight."

The judge cleared his throat. Lucy knew she had to hurry up. "Maybe it sounds dumb to you," she said, "because I'm just a kid. But you could see everybody came there to fight. And I think everybody should just stop fighting and instead . . . maybe listen to what somebody you disagree with has to say."

There was a moment of silence until everybody realized Lucy had finished. Then she heard applause, from just one person. She looked up and saw that it was her mother. Then others joined in, including the jury, so that the judge had to bang his gavel to stop them. But he didn't seem very angry after all.

EIGHT

In the Desert

JULY 1970

SAM WASN'T SURE WHEN HE REALIZED THIS WAS A mistake. At first, he had just wanted to get away from the commune. He had walked as fast as he could in the direction of the mountains where the sun set every evening.

He knew he would have to cross the desert to get there. The same desert where his father had gone to find himself. Since the desert was so flat, with hardly anything growing there but cactus, Sam figured he would eventually be able to spot the place where his father was.

It didn't work out that way. In less than an hour Sam began to feel thirsty. He thought of

97

turning back then, but it looked like the mountains were not much farther away than the commune. It would be cool there, and he could find water. Even in the summer, there was snow high up near the peaks.

But after the sun had risen high in the sky, Sam realized that had been a mistake too. Only now, when he turned to look back at the commune, he could no longer see it.

That didn't matter, Sam told himself. Any minute now, he'd find his father. Dad would have some water and food, or know how to find some.

After another hour, Sam knew that the most important thing now was finding something–anything–to drink. His throat was so dry, he could hardly swallow, and he noticed that he was having trouble walking in a straight line.

He remembered listening to one of the commune members talk about survival tactics in the desert. At the time, what Sam found most interesting was that you could trap small animals like mice or lizards and eat them. You could start a fire by focusing the sun's rays through a piece of glass.

But Sam didn't need a fire, and if there were any animals nearby, they had sense enough to get out of the sun.

Then he remembered. If you cut the top off a certain kind of cactus, you could eat the inside, which held a liquid that was good to drink.

But what kind of cactus? Sam didn't want to eat the kind that made you go out of your mind. The kind with a drink inside wasn't supposed to do that, as far as he could remember.

He looked around for cactuses—any kind. There were lots of tiny ones that looked like stones, but Sam thought the right one was bigger than that.

Then he saw one. It was short and squat, looking a little like a barrel. Barrel cactus was its name. He staggered toward it and saw that it was covered with thick, sharp spines. And Sam didn't have a knife to cut it with.

Barrel Cactus

There were deep ridges in between the spines, and Sam tried to slip his fingers into one. But he only succeeded in stabbing himself. He kicked the side of the cactus, but that didn't work either. So, carefully, he began to pluck spines out of the cactus one by one.

Sam was so weak now that he had to sit down. His fingers were slippery with blood, making it hard to grasp the smooth spines.

Finally he cleared enough of the cactus skin so that he could poke it. Even so, it was tough. His fingers hardly made a dent in the side. Angrily, Sam jabbed at it as hard as he could. He saw a small crack, and picked at it with his fingernails.

With a cry of joy, he pushed his hand inside the cactus and pulled off a chunk. He put it to his mouth with both hands, sucking the juice from it. It tasted sweet, but even better, it seemed cool in his mouth. Juice ran down his chin. If Sam had been asked right then, he would have said he'd never tasted anything so good in his life.

After the first chunk came out, breaking off others was easy. Sucking on the third one, Sam decided he'd better stop. Though he was sure this wasn't the crazy kind of cactus, he dimly recalled that you weren't supposed to eat too much of it.

He stood up, still feeling a little wobbly. Some of his strength had returned, but he wasn't sure how far he could walk. The cactus wasn't a substitute for real food.

Sam surveyed the horizon all around him. The mountains seemed as far off as ever. Off to his left, something rose into the air. At first it looked like smoke, but then Sam saw it must be dust or sand.

He puzzled over it. As far as he knew, there was no road across the desert, but the dust cloud appeared to be moving, as if it were made by a truck or car. Unfortunately, it wasn't coming toward Sam.

He decided to walk in that direction. He noticed that the sun was sinking lower in the sky now. In a few hours it would be dark, and Sam had no wish to be out here alone then.

The distance fooled him again. After what seemed like an hour of walking, the dust cloud seemed as far away as ever.

Even worse, Sam was feeling nauseous, sick to his stomach. Probably it was the cactus. He kept feeling as if he had to throw up, but wasn't able to.

More than anything now, he wanted to lie down, curl up in a ball, and hold his stomach. He wanted his mother to bring a cup of hot soup and crumble pieces of homemade bread into it. . . .

He shook his head. He had to keep walking.

Then a frightening new thought occurred to him: What if he found the dust cloud and it turned out to be nothing more than a gust of wind or something else that couldn't help him? Then what was he going to do?

Sam looked up again. Whatever it was, the dust cloud did seem a little closer now. It was real, at any rate. Not a mirage or a dream. If he just kept going, he would reach it, sooner or later. All he had to do was put one foot in front of the other, take another step . . . one foot in front of the other . . .

Sam's eyes opened. Everything was strange. He was in a white room, lying in a bed under a clean, fresh sheet. Someone was sitting on a chair in a corner of the room. His eyes gradually focused on her.

It was a lady, an old lady, not anybody he knew. She was dressed very well, he noticed. She wore a dark blue dress with lace around the collar. A colorful silk scarf was wrapped around her throat.

She was asleep, or at least her head tilted forward and rested on her chest. Sam opened his mouth to say something, and then discovered he couldn't speak.

It frightened him. Maybe this was what it was like to be dead—you could see what was happening, but couldn't talk or move.

With an effort, he raised his arm. It felt like he hadn't moved it in a long time. But he managed to get it high enough so that he could see it. It did move, so probably he wasn't dead.

He looked at his other arm. It had a tube running into it from a bottle hanging on a metal stand. The liquid inside the tube looked clear—not red, like blood.

Gradually he remembered being in the desert. This must be a hospital. But how did he get here? Did his dad find him?

He tried again to speak. This time, a little sound came out. That encouraged him. "Arrrghh," he said, just trying to make a noise so the woman would wake up.

Frustratingly, she didn't. Maybe *she* was dead. But why would anyone put her in a room where—

A nurse looked through the door and met his eyes. She stepped inside. "Well," she said, "how's our little sleepyhead feeling?"

"Arrghh," he replied. He wanted her to answer questions, not ask them.

"You've been dehydrated," she said, "and ate something mildly toxic. But don't worry. You're going to be all right."

He looked toward the woman on the chair. The nurse understood. "Recognize her?" she said with a big smile. "She's been here for two days. I'll bet you're glad to see her. We found her phone number in your pocket."

She came over to Sam's bed and checked the bottle hanging from the stand. "In a couple more days, you can have something to eat," she said. "Just rest for now."

She left. Sam wanted to scream at her. No, he didn't recognize this woman. Who was she?

Then he remembered when he'd put the piece of paper in his pocket. Grandfather told him to call Nell Aldrich if he needed help. Well, in a way that's what happened. Sam took another look at her. Now he was curious as to how she got here. If only she would wake up.

All of a sudden, she did. Her eyelids fluttered and then opened. Sam was surprised at how blue her eyes were. "Oh," she said, when she saw him looking, "did I fall asleep?"

He couldn't answer, so he nodded. The muscles in his neck felt stiff and hard, so he made a face.

"Do you hurt?" she asked.

He shook his head—and then made another face.

She stood and walked over to the bed. Looking down at him, she asked, "Can you talk?"

He sighed and tried again. This time, he managed to make a noise that sounded like "No."

"You know," said Nell, "we're all wondering who you are."

Who I am? Sam was surprised, but then realized he'd never met her. How could she know who he was?

His tongue wouldn't make the sound "s," and he only managed to say, "Tham."

"Tham?" Nell repeated with a puzzled look.

He closed his eyes and made an effort. It hurt his throat a lot, but he whispered, "Grandfather . . ." and then, after a moment, "Jack."

Nell blinked, but seemed to understand. "You're Jack's grandson," she said. "And he gave you my phone number."

Sam nodded with relief.

"Where is he, anyway?" she asked. "They found you in the desert, all alone. You were nearly . . ." She stopped and thought, then looked at Sam again. "Is Jack with your mother?" she asked.

He nodded.

"Are they in trouble?"

This time, his nod was vigorous. Yes, he thought, can you help them?

"I'll be right back," she said. "I'm going to find a telephone."

Two days later, Sam left the hospital and stepped into an air-conditioned limousine. He could barely remember riding in any kind of automobile before. His parents hadn't owned one when they

were students at Berkeley. All the people at the commune said automobiles were a terrible waste of the earth's resources.

It certainly was comfortable, though. Sam didn't even realize before that a car could be air-conditioned. And it also had a little refrigerator filled with drinks and snacks. This was the way to cross the desert, he decided.

Along with Sam and Nell in the backseat was Dick Aldrich, Sam's mother's cousin. He was one of the people Nell had telephoned on the day Sam woke up. Though Dick had to use crutches to get around, it didn't seem to slow him down any. "Dick's very good at arranging things," Nell had told Sam. "I've told him there's a family down here that he might want to include in a film he's making."

The nurses at the hospital weren't too happy when Dick arrived and set up his camera in Sam's hospital room. But when he told them they might be in his movie, the nurses seemed to change their minds.

Sam hadn't been aware how famous Nell was. Doctors and nurses kept coming into his room—supposedly to check on his condition. But he noticed that most of them just wanted Nell's autograph.

Sam had almost never seen television or movies—two more things his parents didn't approve of. Nell told him it was too bad she wasn't doing her television show any longer. "You would have fit in very well as one of my kids on the show," she said.

He didn't say anything, but secretly he was glad he wasn't. Sam thought he'd probably look stupid because there were so many things he didn't know.

One thing he *did* know was very important, however. That was how to find Grandfather. Sam remembered the name of the little town near the commune. After his voice recovered, he told Nell he was sure he could find the road that would take them there.

That was where they were headed now. Sam only hoped they wouldn't be too late.

Prisoner

SEPTEMBER 1970–APRIL 1971

"HE DIDN'T HAVE TO ENLIST," AUNT IRENE SAID FOR at least the thousandth time. "Nixon was going to end the war anyway."

Lucy was glad that Art wasn't there. Because he would certainly have said—for at least the thousandth time—that Nixon had been in office for nearly four years and the war was still going on.

But Art had left again, although this time they knew where he'd gone. After the jury had found him and the other demonstrators not guilty, Grandpop Rocco lent Art the money to go to the University of Wisconsin. "Stay out of trouble," Rocco had told him. Art said he was going to get a master's degree in education so he could be a teacher.

Then came the terrible news. Two men in blue air force uniforms arrived at the restaurant just before the evening rush started. Everybody knew what that meant. Aunt Irene started to cry as soon as she saw them. Uncle Tony, who was polishing wine glasses at the bar, dropped one. That made Grandpop Rocco look up from his newspaper, and when he saw the air force officers, his face froze.

Lucy saw all this because she was folding napkins into little tents, just the way Grandmama had taught her. And even she knew—because kids at her school had told her—what it meant when somebody in your family was in the war and two men in uniform showed up at the door.

The two officers said there was still hope Mike was alive. His plane had been shot down, but some of the crew had parachuted before it crashed. "Can they be rescued?" Uncle Tony asked.

"They were over North Vietnam," one of the officers replied. "They would have been taken prisoner."

But there was no way of knowing—not just yet, anyway. President Nixon's adviser, Henry Kissinger, was in Paris for peace talks. One of the things that was wanted was a complete list of American prisoners and permission for them to write to their families. But the peace talks were going slowly.

Henry Kissinger

"If only we knew one way or the other," Aunt Irene kept saying. At first, Lucy didn't think that was right. If they knew Mike was dead, there'd be nothing to hope for. There would just be this empty place at the table and you'd know you would never see him again.

But as the weeks went on, Lucy started to understand. Every time the mail arrived or the phone rang, everybody would tense up. Was there any news?

No. No news.

The rest of the time, everybody walked around as if somebody were very ill in the next room.

Nobody wanted to tell any jokes or talk about anything but the war and the peace talks. They didn't even argue anymore, and for the first time Lucy wished they would. It was as if they all worried that raising their voices might break the dishes or something.

Then, one morning Grandpop held up his copy of the *Chicago Tribune* and said, "They're going to release the names of the prisoners."

Everybody crowded around. "Where's the list?" said Uncle Tony. "Is Mike on it?"

"There's no list yet," said Grandpop crossly. He pulled the newspaper away. "They just agreed to provide one."

Now it was even harder to wait. Finally, just before Christmas, the phone rang. Lucy answered it because she was the only one near the reservation desk. A man's voice asked for a relative of Michelangelo Vivanti. She was surprised to hear someone call him by his real name, but replied, "I'm his cousin."

The man paused. "Is there any closer relative there?"

As it happened, Uncle Tony was at the fish market and Aunt Irene had gone to the dentist. "There's my grandfather," Lucy said.

"Could I speak to him?"

The back of Lucy's neck was tingling as she put the phone down and ran to find Grandpop.

She didn't know why, but she was sure the man was calling to say Mike's name was on the prisoner of war list.

Grandpop was tasting some olive oil samples in the kitchen. When Lucy told him about the phone call, he moved faster than Lucy thought he could. She followed and listened as he picked up the phone. He said nothing except, "Yes. Yes, I am. Yes, I understand," but the expression on his face told her what she wanted to know.

He hung up and clapped his hands around her face. "Mike's on the list," he said. "And if all goes well . . . he'll be home soon."

Lucy let out a whoop that woke up two of the waiters.

That evening the Vivantis' dinner table was as lively as ever. Lucy got to tell over and over what the man on the phone had said to her, and how she guessed that Mike was coming home at last.

Only it turned out to be more difficult than they thought. The list of prisoners had come from the peace talks that were still going on in Paris. The United States wanted all the prisoners released before it pulled its troops out of Vietnam.

Everybody thought that would happen soon. It looked like all the sides in the war were ready to stop fighting. And in August the newspapers said that the last American combat troops had left Vietnam.

Yet the prisoners still didn't come home. "I don't understand what's happening," said Grandpop one morning as he looked at the newspaper. "Why won't they let Mike go? That was part of the agreement, wasn't it?"

"It's because the South Vietnamese won't accept the agreement," said Uncle Tony.

"The South? I thought we're supposed to be fighting to protect them," said Grandpop. "It's the North that has the prisoners, isn't it?"

"Right, Pop. But we're still bombing North Vietnam to protect the South. So that's why they won't let the prisoners go."

"I thought Nixon took all of our troops out."

"He took out the ground troops, but we still have all our B-52s over there, like the one Mike

got shot down in. And we're using them to bomb North Vietnam."

"So the North Vietnamese will just take more prisoners if they shoot down our planes?"

"All the time."

Grandpop threw the newspaper down in disgust. "They're all crazy," he said. "We should never have gotten involved in Vietnam in the first place."

That's what Art always said, thought Lucy. But of course she didn't say that aloud.

Christmas wasn't very merry that year. The Vivantis decorated the interior of the restaurant with lights and a tree, just like always. But everybody was worried about Mike. Aunt Irene would suddenly excuse herself and go into the kitchen to cry. Grandpop even talked about retiring and moving to Florida, the way Grandmama always said she wanted to do.

And Art didn't come home from the University of Wisconsin for Christmas. Nixon had increased the bombing just before Christmas. Lucy saw on TV pictures of protests against the bombing at colleges around the country. She figured that was what Art must be doing, even though he'd promised he wouldn't, after he got out of jail.

New Year's came, and everybody made a wish at midnight. Lucy didn't need to ask what people

wished for this year. They were all hoping for the same thing.

Then, in January, after the Christmas lights came down and the streets were filled with snow and ice, there was a news bulletin on TV. Lucy was upstairs doing her homework while watching television. A news broadcaster broke in to announce that the president would give an address to the nation at eight o'clock.

She went downstairs to tell her parents, but everybody in the restaurant had already heard the news. By eight o'clock people were gathered around the television sets in the cocktail lounge. President Nixon appeared in the screen. He always looked tense to Lucy, but this time more than ever. Lucy didn't like him because he looked like a person who never had any fun.

"My fellow Americans," he began, as he always did. As he went on, it became clear that a peace agreement had been reached. The war was over!

But was it, really? Lucy looked around the room. Nobody was cheering, or even smiling. She'd heard Grandpop tell about the end of World War II, when there were parades and he'd kept the restaurant open all night just because people wanted to celebrate.

Now . . . there was no celebration. Of course, the country had been told several times before that the war was over, or almost over. So maybe they just wanted to wait and see.

Hesitantly, Lucy went over to where Grandpop was sitting. She put her arm around him. "Grandpop," she said, "this means Mike's coming home, doesn't it?"

"I hope so," was all he said.

Nobody knew what would happen next. Uncle Tony tried to call somebody in the Defense Department who knew about the prisoners. But he couldn't find out anything.

The newspapers said that all the prisoners would be flown to an American air force base in the Philippines. "Maybe we should go out there," said Aunt Irene.

"It's a long way," said Uncle Tony, "and we don't know when he'll arrive. The North Vietnamese have sixty days to send everybody back."

"So what happens after they reach the Philippines?" asked Lucy's father.

"If they need medical care, they'll stay there," said Uncle Tony. He clenched his fists. "There are rumors that some of them were tortured, or have . . . you know, lost their minds."

Everybody sat and thought about that. Aunt Irene went to the kitchen.

A few days later, somebody finally called from the Defense Department. He said the Vivantis would be notified when Mike arrived in the Philippines. So once again, they waited.

Days went by and nothing happened. Then, on a freezing cold day in the middle of February, the door to the restaurant opened. Lucy was waiting for the delivery truck to bring fresh eggplants that Grandpop had ordered from a farm in Italy. She had just looked at the clock and saw that the time was four o'clock. Feeling the breeze from the doorway, she turned.

But it wasn't the delivery man. It was somebody wearing a blue uniform. An air force uniform. Lucy stared. At first, it didn't look like him. Not at all. He had lost a lot of weight and his face had changed. He had always had a smile for her, for everybody.

"Mike?" she said.

He looked at her, and she wanted to run away because his eyes were so full of hurt.

"Hey, Loose," he said. That was his pet name for her. "Surprised to see me? They wanted me to go in the hospital, but I told them the only medicine I wanted was some of Grandmama's lasagna. I snagged a seat on a plane to the States, and didn't have time to call. What's that I smell cooking?"

Just then, his mother came through the kitchen door. Aunt Irene screamed and dropped the tray of silverware she was carrying. Then she stared, just like Lucy had. "Mike, aw Mikey," she yelled. "What did they do to you?"

That brought everybody else who was in the restaurant at the time. Gabriella, Grandpop, Grandmama, Isabel, and Lucy's mother. All of them reacted the same way. They hugged Mike and told him how glad they were he was home. But they shot glances at him when they thought he wasn't looking.

"What's the matter with everybody?" Grandpop said. "Look at him! He hasn't had a decent meal in a year, I'll bet. Sit down, Mike. We're gonna give you the best feast you ever had. Gabriella, where's that special wine I've been saving?"

"Oh, no wine, Grandpop," said Mike. "The docs said I had malaria and can't drink alcohol for a while."

"No wine?" Rocco looked aghast. He shook his head and went into the kitchen.

Uncle Tony and Lucy's father soon arrived, and when they saw Mike, they got angry. "You see my boy?" Tony kept asking the waiters. "That's what they did to him over in Vietnam." If he could have, Lucy thought, Uncle Tony would go back and make the Vietnamese sorry for what they'd done.

Everybody seemed to want Mike to make up that evening for every one of the meals he'd missed. Whenever he said he couldn't eat any more, one of the Vivantis would rush out to the kitchen to make something he couldn't turn down.

Since Mike couldn't drink wine, Rocco and Uncle Tony tried to make up for it by drinking twice as much as usual. They were talking pretty loudly by ten o'clock, when somebody else walked through the front door.

It was Art. Lucy was the only one who wasn't surprised. She had telephoned him that afternoon to tell him Mike was home.

Gradually everybody fell silent. There was an awkward feeling in the room. Mike struggled to his feet and held out his hand. Art rushed to grasp it, and then the two of them hugged.

"You were right," Lucy heard Mike say.

"Nah, you were right," Art replied.

The phone rang, and Gabriella went to answer it. "It's another reporter," she called out. The newspapers had been calling all evening, wanting to interview Mike.

"Hang up," Rocco told her. "We don't want to talk about the war anymore," he said. "Tell them the war is over."

Wishes Granted

OCTOBER 1971

LATER ON, WHEN SAM WAS AT SCHOOL, HE dreamed about the day he went back to the commune. Some of the things he dreamed were true, but others weren't. When he awoke, he thought maybe this was what it was like when people ate the dried cactus.

"We've been worried about your grandfather," Nell had explained on the way. "Before he disappeared, the doctors told him he hadn't long to live."

Sam nodded. He remembered Grandfather saying he didn't have much time to teach things to Sam.

"Because of his work in the antiwar movement," Nell continued, "there were FBI agents following him all the time. It annoyed him, and one day he gave them the slip. Gave everybody the slip, because he just vanished without telling anybody where he was going."

"I know," Sam said. "He sort of told me that when he arrived. I guess he hitchhiked and walked."

"Well, we all thought he was going to try to find your mother. But of course, nobody knew exactly where *she* was either."

Nell sighed. "Maybe it would have been better if everybody in the family had stayed at my grandfather's house in Maine. But of course, families aren't like that anymore."

Sam was interested. "Mother mentioned that house once. Do you still own it?"

She nodded. "I think we all own part of it. You will probably inherit your part someday, unless it's sold."

"I hope nobody ever sells it," Sam said. "At least not before I get to see it."

"Well, first things first," said Nell. "We've got to locate your grandfather and see if he wants help."

"He needs help for sure," said Sam. "The last time I saw him, he was in the sweat lodge and nobody could wake him up."

"I said if he wants help, not needs help," Nell replied. "I think that once he found you and your mother, he may have finished everything he wanted to do."

The air-conditioning suddenly felt chilly. Sam shivered. He felt lonely. His father was still gone, his grandfather might be dead, and his mother . . .

Nell was talking about her now. "Esther was a brilliant student. She seemed to want to make up for the loss of her brother by becoming twice as good as anybody else." She looked out the window and paused.

"Perhaps that was a mistake," Nell said softly. "At some point, carrying that burden became too much for her."

"Grandfather wanted her to go back to college," Sam said.

"That's because he thought that would make her happy. But who knows? Maybe this . . . commune life is better for her. It's hard to know, when you're young, what you really ought to do."

"I know what I want to do," said Sam.

She smiled at him. "And what's that?"

"I want to go to a real school, and then a college, and learn everything I can."

Nell nodded. "You can do that. I'll help you."

For some reason, Sam recalled what Grandfather had told him when he gave him Nell's telephone number: "Be careful what you ask for. You might get it." Sam felt as if he had just stepped into a new place, and realized he couldn't go back to the old one ever again.

The limousine reached the little town near the commune, and the driver stopped to ask Sam for directions.

"There's a little road that turns to the left after the gas station," Sam told him. "Follow that until you see a fork in the road. And then go left again."

The car traveled more slowly now, because the road kept getting worse. Suddenly Sam sat upright and pointed out the window. A cloud of dust or sand was rising into the sky, just like the one he'd seen in the desert. He hadn't thought of it till now.

"See that?" he said. "What is that?"

Dick spoke up from the other side of the car. "It's a mining exploration," he said. "They're drilling in the ground, looking for copper."

"I guess you don't remember," said Nell. "It was one of those drilling teams that found you."

"I really don't remember," he said. "I didn't even know there were any mines around here."

"There aren't," said Dick. "But the geologists think there may be copper in the ground. I read a newspaper article about it. If they find it, this area is going to change a lot."

Sam was silent. The people of the commune had settled out here because they wanted to be far away from civilization. "We'll never be bothered," he remembered his dad saying, "because nobody else wants this land."

"Why were you out in the desert by yourself, anyway?" asked Nell.

"I was looking for my dad," Sam replied. "He went to find himself. He does that sometimes."

Sam saw Nell and Dick exchange glances. They seemed to know something they didn't want him to know.

"What is it?" Sam asked. "Do you know anything about where my dad went?"

Nell squeezed his hand. "The miners who found you said that they'd also seen a man wandering in the desert. They offered to take him into town, but he refused. The miners thought . . . well, they thought he couldn't survive out there."

"They don't know my dad," said Sam firmly. "He could."

Just then, he saw the turnoff for the commune. "Go down that little road on the left!" he called to the driver.

It wasn't long after that till they came in sight of the old ranch house and the other buildings the commune had built around it. They looked different to Sam now than they had before. Somehow they had become shabby and rundown. Or maybe they'd always been that way, and Sam was only seeing them the way he imagined Nell and Dick did.

Some kind of ceremony was going on. Sam could see a plume of smoke rising from the field where the commune members gathered to pay homage to nature. The limousine pulled to a stop at the ranch house, and everyone got out.

Nell sniffed the air. "What's that burning?" she asked.

"LuAnn adds herbs to the fire on special occasions," Sam replied.

As they walked toward the smoke, they heard singing. It wasn't the mournful, scary chant of the sweat lodge. It sounded more like a song of celebration and joy.

As Sam turned the corner of the ranch house, he saw that everybody was circling the fire, hand in hand. It was a big fire, made with logs they probably should have saved for the winter. Nobody noticed Sam and the others until they had nearly reached the circle. Then LuAnn pointed to them. People's heads turned. The circle broke and the dancing and chanting slowed and finally stopped.

Everybody stared. Sam felt awkward, but then he realized they weren't staring at him. One of the men took a few shy steps forward. "Aunt Nell?" he asked.

Nell gave him a little wave and a smile. The man turned and said to the others, "Oh, wow. It's Aunt Nell."

The fire seemed forgotten as everybody gathered around Nell. Sam searched the faces of the crowd for his mother. He didn't see her.

Agatha, still the leader, stepped forward. "Aunt Nell, we welcome you. Have you come to join our celebration of the life of our brother?"

Sam's heart sank. That must mean Grandfather had . . .

"You mean Jack Aldrich?" asked Nell.

"That was his earthly name."

"He was my cousin. I came here looking for him."

That news went through the crowd like a strong wind in a cornfield. The commune members even made a noise . . . oooooooh . . . that sounded like a breeze blowing.

One of those closest to Nell suddenly dropped to his knees. Sam jumped back, because it frightened him. Then two or three more people knelt, and finally the whole crowd.

Nell gave a little bow as if this happened to her all the time. "All right, now," she said, clapping her hands. "It's not nap time, you know, children. Let's go on with the ceremony. I'm sure Jack would like that."

She walked through the crowd, helping each person stand up again.

"That's the way she did it on the show when nap time was over," Dick told Sam in a low voice. He started to set up his camera.

In a few moments, the group was circling the fire again. Sam felt someone take his hand. He looked and saw his mother's face. She smiled serenely at him as if she had never noticed he had gone away.

A year had gone by since all that happened. Sam was dreaming about it as his alarm clock went off. He pulled the covers over his head, not wanting to leave the dream. He knew that if he were there in the commune just a second longer he would feel somebody take his other hand and when he turned, he would see his father.

"Gotta get up for the run, Nerd." That was his roommate, Brian. He didn't think it was good for Sam to study so much. Brian was into sports.

Sometimes Sam wished he hadn't come here to Rigley School. Nell suggested it because her nephew Charley had come here, and so had his son Chuck. According to Nell, they had enjoyed every minute of it. For somebody used to living outdoors, like Sam, it would be a great place.

Except, of course, that ever since November there had been snow on the ground and it was freezing cold outside. It was nothing like the weather in Arizona at the commune.

Sam sighed and tossed off the blankets. The shock of cold air in the room—Brian said it was healthy to sleep with the window open—woke him up. His feet touched the floor, which felt like a frozen lake.

No sense thinking about the commune, because that was all gone now. When a vein of copper was discovered on the land, the members voted to sell it and go somewhere else to get in touch with the spirits of nature.

Nell offered to let them move near Aldrich House in Maine. Some of them were there now, but most of the others took their share of the money and scattered to different places.

Sam's mother was one of those at Aldrich House. Nell's friend Dr. Tamura was taking care of her. He said she just needed some time to relax and recuperate.

Sam pulled on his sweat suit and jogging shoes. He thought again of his grandfather's warning. Sam had gotten his wish—he wanted to go to school and here he was. And there was no doubt about it—he was learning a lot.

But he missed everybody in the commune, even Agatha. Most of all, he missed his dad. The last thing Sam did before he left was to write a message on the wall of the ranch house. So if Dad ever came back, he'd know where Sam and his mother had gone.

Every day since then, Sam had secretly hoped to hear from his dad. A letter, a phone call . . . something. Sam knew that Dad would get in touch, and then they could all be together again.

"Ready?" Brian said.

Sam stood up and followed Brian outside, where the air was full of snowflakes. They were falling so heavily that it was hard to see. Sam saw that the other boys had started to gather by the trees, and then he heard someone call his name.

Sam turned around. Standing there next to a corner of the residence hall was his dad. He held out his arms, and Sam ran to him. "I knew you'd come back," Sam said. "I *knew* it."

"You weren't so easy to track down," Dad said.

"Didn't you see the address I left on the ranch house?"

"Yes, but that only brought me to Maine. That old lady . . . Nell. She's pretty careful about who she gives information to."

"But you're my dad! She'd have to tell you where I was."

"Not till we had a long talk. She wanted to make sure I wasn't going to take you out of this school."

Sam hesitated. "Are you?"

"Do you like it here?"

"Yeah, it's . . . sort of what I want. For now."

"Then Nell's right. You should stay."

"Are you going to live around here?"

Dad shook his head. "I decided to go back to school too."

"You did? Why?"

"I don't know. I guess I finally looked deeply enough into myself. I'm ready to study something else now."

"Are you going back to Berkeley?"

"Probably. But don't worry. I'll be back to see you. Nell said we can spend summers at her place in Maine."

A whistle blew. Sam looked over to see the gym teacher gesturing. "I've got to go run now," Sam said. "Will you be here when we get back?"

"Sure," his dad said.

"You promise?"

"Yes, don't worry. I won't go wandering off."

"Because I've got a lot to tell you."

"I want to hear it too."

Sam took off then, hurrying to catch up with the others. He took a last look over his shoulder to see if his dad was still there. He was, and looked strange with the snowflakes starting to cover his parka. Sam began to run faster. He had to finish the run and get back before his dad went wandering again.

The
Movie

JUNE 1973

"GRANDPOP, IT'S TIME TO GO," LUCY CALLED.

There was no answer. He was probably glued to the television, watching the Watergate hearings. They seemed to be on TV all the time now. All the stations too, cutting off some of Lucy's favorite afternoon programs.

Sometimes Grandpop would get angry at what he was watching and turn the set off. But he turned it back on in a few minutes, because he couldn't stand to miss anything.

So far, the committee hadn't found out anything really bad about the president himself. Of course it was hard for Lucy to tell. The Vivantis

135

Watergate hearings

argued about the Watergate affair a lot at the dinner table. Art thought Nixon would be impeached. Lucy's father thought the Democrats were just out to get the president. Rocco was bothered a lot by the thought that the president might have broken the law. That was why he was glued to the television.

Today, however, there was something a lot more important going on. At least Lucy thought so. It was the premiere of Dick's movie. Two weeks ago an engraved invitation had arrived, inviting the whole Vivanti family.

Lucy thought at first that some of her relatives might still be upset with Dick. But all that had been forgotten, or at least forgiven. Because who could resist the chance to go see themselves in a movie?

Apparently, Rocco could. And maybe Grandmama too. Everybody else in the family had already left for the screening. Lucy had to stay late at school for a music lesson that day, so she volunteered to make sure Grandpop remembered to come. He wouldn't leave until the Watergate hearings were over for the day.

Grandmama had been invited too, but she had gone upstairs complaining that she had a headache. Lucy suspected that what really bothered Grandmama was the news that Nell Aldrich was going to be at the premiere. Lucy's mother had told her, "I think your Nonna is still a little jealous. She only gets these headaches when Nell comes to Chicago."

Lucy found it hard to believe. Grandpop and Grandmama had celebrated their fiftieth wedding anniversary a year ago. And if you were married that long . . . how could you be jealous?

Well, no matter if Grandmama wanted to come or not—Lucy had to get Grandpop there. For one thing, she didn't want to miss any of the film.

Marshall Field's Department store

Mom had taken her to Marshall Field's, where Lucy had bought a new skirt and sweater outfit. "Don't let your father see how short that skirt is," Mom had told Lucy. "Not till the premiere, anyway." Daddy didn't understand that miniskirts were in.

Lucy peeked into the cocktail lounge and saw that the television was still on. She could see that a soap opera was on, though, so maybe the hearings were over for the day. She went over to the upholstered leather chair that Grandpop liked to sit in.

He was asleep. Lucy sighed. He didn't like anybody to wake him. Some nights lately, he would stay in this chair all night after the restaurant closed. "There's no law that says you have to lie down to sleep," he told his family.

But Lucy knew he wanted to see the movie. So she jiggled his arm a little bit. He didn't respond, so she tried again, harder this time.

His eyelids flickered, and he mumbled something. Then he said it again, very distinctly: "Nell? Is that you?"

"Grandpop!" Lucy called loudly, "It's me, Lucy!"

He looked at her strangely. His eyes were very far away, but gradually focused. "Oh, sure," he said. "What's the matter, Lucy? Why'd you wake me up?"

"It's time to go to the premiere, Grandpop. You told me to remind you."

"Oh, sure." He ran his fingers through his gray hair. "We can't miss that."

As he struggled to his feet, Lucy asked, "Why'd you think I was Nell, Grandpop?"

"Who said I thought you were Nell?"

"You called me Nell just then." She giggled. "Were you dreaming about her?"

He grunted and said, "What you dream is what you dream. What time is it?"

In the end Grandmama decided to go along. Lucy knew she would, because she must be curious. Dick's movie was going to be on television, instead of in theaters. So the premiere screening was scheduled to be in a hotel ballroom.

When they arrived, Lucy was relieved to find that they weren't too late. The room was pretty much filled, however. Folding chairs had been set up in front of a big screen. Lucy looked around for her family. Then she saw her father waving at her from way up front.

The Vivantis had saved three seats. "How did you manage to do that?" asked Lucy, as she sat down next to her father. "There are hardly any empty seats in the whole room."

"We're the stars of the movie, remember?" her father said. "These are reserved for us."

Oh sure, Lucy thought. Then a sinking feeling came over her. Up till that moment she had felt watching the movie would be fun. Then she realized that a whole bunch of strangers would see it too—not to mention a couple million people who would watch it on TV.

And what they would see . . . was Lucy's family just the way they really were. Or at least the way Dick wanted people to see them. As the lights went down, and the buzz of conversation quieted, Lucy had the terrifying feeling that she didn't want to see this. At all.

She relaxed a little because the beginning wasn't too bad. Dick showed the outside of the restaurant and the little brass plaque that said it had been run by the Vivanti family since 1924. The camera moved inside the restaurant to show that it was empty, but Lucy knew it wouldn't stay that way for long.

Sure enough, the scene shifted to the kitchen and there was Gabriella at the stove. She looked good, even in an apron and chef's hat. Gabriella gave a little history of the restaurant and the family. As she did, the camera panned around some of the still photographs that were on the walls of the restaurants. Finally, it settled on a photo of the Vivanti family seated around the dinner table. The camera paused on each of their faces while Gabriella introduced them.

Lucy felt a little cheated. Why should Gabriella get to be the narrator? That wasn't going to go over with Uncle Tony and Lucy's father. Both of them wanted to run the restaurant when Grandpop finally retired.

Anyway, now the family part of the movie began. The still picture of the Vivantis suddenly came alive, and of course there was an argument going on. Lucy cringed to think how the audience would react to this.

And then the camera showed her, talking loud and arguing just like the rest of them. This wasn't fair! She hardly ever argued. Dick must have taken the one time out of thousands of hours that Lucy actually spoke up.

And her voice? Did she really sound like that? Or look that bad? Why didn't somebody tell her to brush her hair?

She sank into her seat, trying not to think how horrible this looked. Oh, my gosh! When the film was shown on television, everybody in her school could see it.

One thing Lucy *was* curious about, however. As the movie focused more on Art and Mike, she remembered the riot in the park. At last she would get to see the film Dick took that day and find out just who it was . . .

But he skipped it! Or most of it anyway. There were just a few seconds left, showing Art in his flag shirt, waving a sign. If you didn't know the whole story, you wouldn't realize where it was.

Lucy looked around to see where Dick was sitting. She wanted to ask why he'd left out the most important part. But she didn't see him.

Meanwhile, the story of the Vivanti family came to an end. Only that wasn't the end of the movie. Now came part two, and the screen showed a very different place. It looked like a farm.

There was a different narrator too—some woman who called herself Agatha. She described how all the people living in this place had come together to be "a family of the spirit," whatever that meant. Anyway, Lucy could see they were a bunch of hippies. This was the kind of place Art might have wound up in, if he hadn't gone to college.

They were sort of sweet, though. It was probably fun to grow your own food and run around barefoot all day. One of the main characters in this part of the film was a boy around Lucy's age. Sam was his name. He was cute, she thought, a little like Huckleberry Finn, only sad. She wished somebody would cheer him up.

There was a lot of arguing going on among this family too, even if they were hippies. They had to decide whether to sell their land or stay there. Everybody started off sounding nice and reasonable, but in the end they got angry just like the Vivantis.

In the third section of the film, Dick himself was the narrator. He explained that he'd taken some of the film in this part when his father was alive. Also, he had interviewed people like his father's brother Jack and cousin Peggy before they died. "I wanted to know what my family was like," he explained.

This part of the film was in some ways the most interesting, Lucy thought. For one thing, Dick included scenes from old movies that his father had starred in. He even had some footage of his father driving in automobile races a long time ago.

At first, it was sad to compare those pictures with the sight of Dick's father after he got sick. Seeing this old man in a wheelchair, hardly able to speak made Lucy wonder if getting old was always bad.

Although . . . when Dick's father, Harry Aldrich, *did* speak, Lucy got the feeling that he still enjoyed life. He was helping his son make this movie, and had made another as well. Even though he couldn't do sword fights on the deck of burning ships any longer, he was still the same person inside.

All the other people Dick interviewed had stories too. Dick had gone to France, where his mother lived now. She seemed unhappy to be on camera talking about her husband. And Dick even tracked down two more of his father's cousins— Molly and Polly. They were pretty old too, but you could see they were twins. One was a retired professor and the other a physical health instructor at a retirement home. They remembered how, as children, they had shared summers at the house in Maine with Harry and his brother Jack. It sounded like fun.

Jack spoke too, and Nell came on screen of course, and her sister Peggy . . . and all of them had something to say.

Somehow, Lucy thought, it was sort of confusing. Dick was trying to find out what his father was really like. But it turned out to be very hard to discover that. The very last part of the movie showed Dick talking with his father, asking him questions. But Harry didn't remember everything Dick wanted to know.

Lucy suddenly realized what was wrong: In the first two parts of the movie, Dick had filmed other people's families. In this part, he was trying to understand his own. But because he was part of it, he couldn't see it as well. It was like trying to take a picture of a house when you were inside the house.

When the movie ended, everybody in her family stood up and applauded. All the Vivantis thought their family was the best, and they were sure others would see it that way too. They didn't think they looked silly, even with all their arguing.

So Lucy stopped worrying. She clapped her hands along with the rest. Across the aisle she spotted the boy named Sam. He'd gotten new clothes—a school blazer and tie—and even wore shoes. At the party afterward, she would see if he wanted to talk, or was a dork like all the boys in her class at school.

On the other side of her, Grandpop was saying something to Grandmama. Lucy leaned close so she could hear. Maybe she'd learn why Grandmama was jealous of Nell.

But what she heard was Rocco saying, "Compared to those hippies, Art didn't look so bad, did he?"

A Few Historical Notes

The Vietnam War divided Americans in a way no other war ever has. Sadly, the United States need never have become involved in a conflict that caused the deaths of 58,000 Americans and more than a million people in South Vietnam. American involvement began when the Vietnamese defeated the French, who had formerly colonized the country. The 1954 peace agreement that gave Vietnam its independence guaranteed that free elections would be held the following year. But as U.S. president Dwight Eisenhower wrote in his memoirs, his administration decided not to allow free elections because the Vietnamese leader Ho Chi Minh would almost certainly win—and Ho was a Communist. A U.S.-backed leader was installed in the southern part of Vietnam, and Ho ruled the North.

From that point on, the Americans sent military advisers and then troops, equipment, ships, and planes to prop up our "allies" in South Vietnam. President Lyndon Johnson sent more than half a million young Americans to fight in Vietnam, but it was clear that the Vietcong rebels in the South, as well as the people of North Vietnam, could not be defeated.

The rising casualty lists caused some Americans to protest against the government's policies. The right-wing media and prowar politicians accused them of disloyalty. The protests grew more numerous and, sometimes, violent. In May 1970, four students were killed by National Guardsmen at Kent State University in Ohio. The guardsmen had fired at demonstrators, and some of the students who were wounded and killed were merely walking across the campus.

One of the largest antiwar demonstrations took place in Chicago in late August 1968, during the Democratic National Convention. Thousands of protesters came to the city to show their opposition to the war. Chicago police reacted with violence; knowing that the actions of the police were being televised, demonstrators chanted, "The whole world's watching."

The Democrats nominated vice president Hubert Humphrey for president. His opponent, Republican Richard Nixon, promised that he had a "secret plan" to end the war. Nixon won, but the United States continued to be involved in the war for five more years. The peace terms finally agreed to in Paris in 1973 were only a face-saving way for the United States to leave Vietnam. Two years later, the Vietnamese Communists defeated the remaining opposition forces, and Vietnam became one country, as it is today.

The rebellious spirit that began in the late 1960s continued through the 1970s. Following the lead of the black civil rights movement, other groups began to work for greater equality in American life. Women, Latinos, and gay Americans all started to organize liberation groups during the 1970s.

Some Americans showed their distrust for society by "dropping out" altogether. Groups of people attempted to live self-sufficiently by banding together to grow their own food and live a communal lifestyle, in which work was shared. The commune in this story is not based on any particular one of these. Whether they failed or succeeded, those who chose this way of life did so out of idealism.

Watergate was the name given to a series of scandals and crimes that eventually caused President Richard Nixon to resign—the only president to do so. The name came from the Watergate Hotel in Washington, D.C., where the Democratic National Committee had its headquarters. Late one night in June 1972, a group of burglars were caught there, and it was discovered that they were working for the Committee to Re-Elect the President [Nixon]. This led to congressional investigations and the appointment of a special prosecutor to investigate Nixon's misconduct in office. After nearly a year of new revelations, Nixon chose to resign rather than face what appeared to be certain impeachment. Nixon's successor, President Gerald Ford, pardoned him for any crimes he had committed while in office.

THE ALDRICH

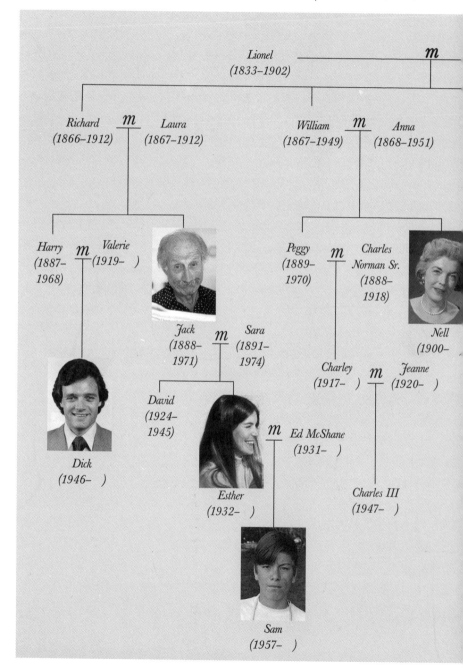

Lionel
(1833–1902)

m

Richard
(1866–1912)
m
Laura
(1867–1912)

William
(1867–1949)
m
Anna
(1868–1951)

Harry
(1887–1968)
m
Valerie
(1919–)

Peggy
(1889–1970)
m
Charles
Norman Sr.
(1888–1918)

Nell
(1900–

Jack
(1888–1971)
m
Sara
(1891–1974)

Charley
(1917–)
m
Jeanne
(1920–)

David
(1924–1945)

Esther
(1932–)
m
Ed McShane
(1931–)

Charles III
(1947–)

Dick
(1946–)

Sam
(1957–)

FAMILY

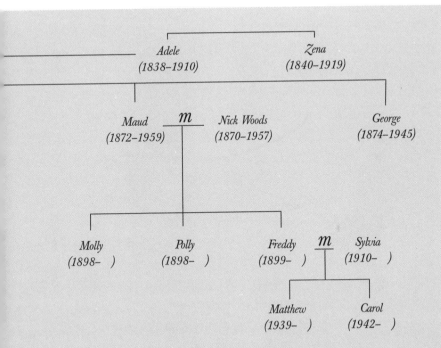

Adele
(1838–1910)

Zena
(1840–1919)

Maud
(1872–1959)

_m_

Nick Woods
(1870–1957)

George
(1874–1945)

Molly
(1898–)

Polly
(1898–)

Freddy
(1899–)

_m_

Sylvia
(1910–)

Matthew
(1939–)

Carol
(1942–)

THE VIVANTI FAMILY

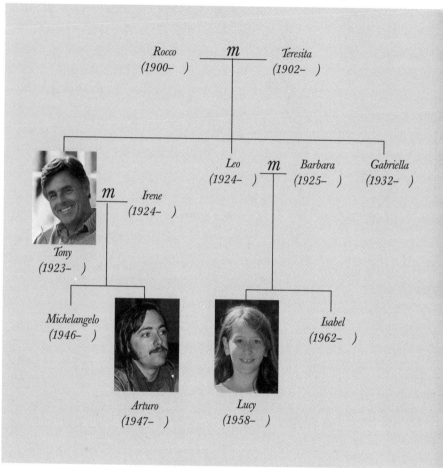

Rocco *(1900–)* **m** Teresita *(1902–)*

Tony *(1923–)* **m** Irene *(1924–)*

Leo *(1924–)* **m** Barbara *(1925–)*

Gabriella *(1932–)*

Michelangelo *(1946–)*

Arturo *(1947–)*

Lucy *(1958–)*

Isabel *(1962–)*

THE DIXON FAMILY

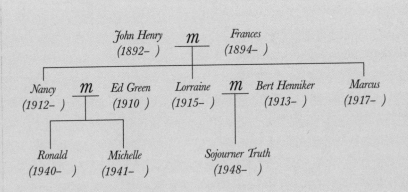

John Henry (1892–) _m_ Frances (1894–)

Nancy (1912–) _m_ Ed Green (1910)

Lorraine (1915–) _m_ Bert Henniker (1913–)

Marcus (1917–)

Ronald (1940–)

Michelle (1941–)

Sojourner Truth (1948–)

Things That Really Happened

1970

On April 22 the first Earth Day was celebrated to encourage people to increase their efforts to fight pollution of the environment.

During an antiwar protest at Kent State University in Ohio on May 4, National Guard troops fire at a crowd of students, killing four.

1971

The smiley face on a yellow background appears almost everywhere, starting with pin-back buttons.

The 26th Amendment to the Constitution, lowering the voting age from 21 to 18, is ratified.

1972

On February 21, President Richard Nixon visits Beijing, China, for talks with Mao Zedong and other Communist Chinese leaders. Nixon is the first president ever to visit China. In May he becomes the first president to visit Moscow, the capital of the Soviet Union.

On June 17, five men later found to be working for President Nixon's re-election campaign are arrested for breaking into the Democratic National Headquarters in the Watergate Hotel in Washington, D.C.

"Pong," the first computer-chip video game, makes its appearance.

President Nixon wins reelection over Senator George McGovern in a landslide victory. Just before the election,

During the Years 1970-1979

the president's national security adviser, Henry Kissinger, announced that peace talks in Paris were going well and that "peace is at hand."

At the end of December, Nixon launches the most devastating bombing attacks of the war on North Vietnam's major cities. News of the deaths of civilians and destruction of hospitals brought renewed protests by Americans against the war.

1973

A peace agreement between the United States, South Vietnam, the Viet Cong, and North Vietnam is signed in Paris on January 27. The last U.S. military forces leave the country two months later.

Secretariat becomes the first horse in 25 years to win the "Triple Crown," the Kentucky Derby, Preakness, and Belmont Stakes. His rider in all three races was 18.

A special Senate committee begins looking into abuses of power by President Nixon and his aides, in what becomes known as the "Watergate affair." Several of the president's closest aides are forced to resign, and some later were tried and convicted of various charges.

Later, the Senate committee learns that the president taped his conversations in his White House office. When a special prosecutor demands that Nixon release the tapes, he refuses and fires the prosecutor.

On October 10, Vice President Spiro T. Agnew resigns, pleading no contest to charges of tax evasion. Two days later, Gerald Ford is appointed vice president. Both houses of Congress confirm his appointment, and he is sworn in on December 6.

OPEC (Organization of Petroleum Exporting Countries) cuts off shipments of oil to Western nations that supported Israel's occupation of Arab territories. The "Arab oil embargo" created long lines and much higher prices at gas stations in the United States. Though the embargo ended the following year, it emphasized the United States' dependence on foreign oil.

Professional football's Miami Dolphins complete a perfect season of 14 regular-season wins and 3 playoff victories, including the Super Bowl. No other modern NFL team has ever gone undefeated in a season.

1974

On April 8, Hank Aaron of the Atlanta Braves hits his 715th home run, breaking the career record set by Babe Ruth.

On May 9 the House Judiciary Committee opens impeachment hearings against President Nixon. At the end of July, it recommended that the House adopt three articles of impeachment against the president.

The Supreme Court rules that the president must give up the tapes of his White House conversations. When he does, the tapes indicate that he conspired to obstruct the investigation into the Watergate burglary. Obstruction of justice is itself a crime.

Rather than face possible impeachment, President Nixon announces his resignation on August 8 and leaves office the next day on August 9. Two hours later, Gerald R. Ford is sworn in as the 38th president. Because he was appointed to fill the vice presidency, Ford is the first president not to be elected to either office. A month later,

Ford pardoned President Nixon for any federal crimes he may have committed while in office.

1975

In April, Communist forces complete their victory over the South Vietnamese government. The last American civilians and some South Vietnamese are evacuated by helicopter in a rush to safety.

Robert Chandler, a custom-car builder from Missouri, displays his "Bigfoot," a souped-up Ford truck with four-foot-high tires. This was the first of the "monster trucks." Later, monster truck rallies—in which the giant vehicles rolled over lesser, ordinary vehicles—attracted crowds.

The home video cassette player-recorder is introduced.

Mood rings become popular. They display a heat-sensitive liquid crystal that changes color to reflect the wearer's shifting moods.

The pet rock becomes a fad. Dreamed up by a California ad executive, a pet rock came in a box (with airholes), and instructions on how to teach it to do "tricks." Nudging it would cause it to roll over, and with hardly any encouragement, a pet rock could learn to play dead. Best of all, they were low-maintenance, with no need to feed or walk them. Supposedly, 5 million pet rocks were sold, mostly as gifts.

1976

On July 4 the United States celebrates the Bicentennial, the 200th anniversary of its founding.

Jimmy Carter of Georgia is elected as the nation's 39th president.

1977

The first of George Lucas's *Star Wars* movies is released, and becomes a huge success.

The television miniseries *Roots*, which followed a black family from enslavement in Africa to emancipation after the Civil War, attracts an audience of 130 million viewers, the largest in TV history up to that time. One episode was shown on ABC each night for eight consecutive nights.

1978

California voters approve Proposition 13, which limited property taxes in the state. This was the beginning of a "taxpayers' revolt" that resulted in similar measures in other states.

The first women are chosen for the NASA space program.

1979

The U.S. Mint issues a new one-dollar coin, bearing the likeness of feminist Susan B. Anthony. She is the first real woman to appear on a U.S. coin.

On March 28, a partial nuclear meltdown releases radioactive material at a nuclear reactor at Three Mile Island near Harrisburg, Pennsylvania. The event creates fears about the safety of other nuclear energy plants.

On November 4, 90 people, including 63 Americans, are taken prisoner by militants at the U.S. Embassy in Tehran, Iran. The ruler of Iran, the Muslim cleric Ayatollah Khomeini, demands that the United States return the former Shah of Iran, who is undergoing medical treatment in Los Angeles. The hostages will be held by Iran for 444 days.